Boy,
Howdy!

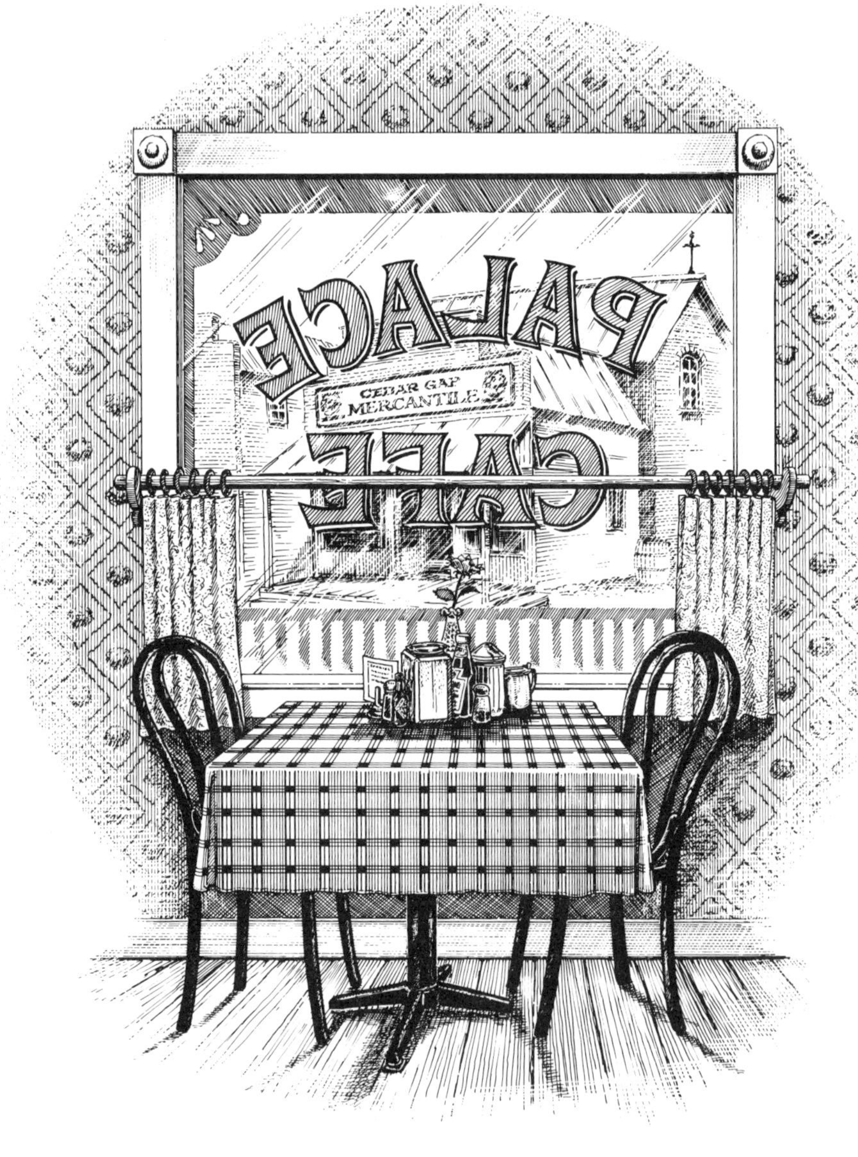
PALACE
CEDAR GAP
MERCANTILE
CAFE

Boy, Howdy!

JACK BOYD

Texas Tech University Press
1990

Volume 2 of the Cedar Gap Archives

Printed in the United States of America

This book was set in 10 on 13 Galliard and printed on acid-free paper that meets
the guidelines for permanence and durability of the Committee on Production
Guidelines for Book Longevity of the Council on Library Resources. ∞

Frontispiece by David Smith
Design by Joanna Hill

Library of Congress Cataloging-in-Publication Data

Boyd, Jack, 1932–
   Boy, howdy! / Jack Boyd.
      p.   cm. — (The Cedar Gap archives ; v. 2)
   ISBN 0-89672-227-9
   1. Texas—Social life and customs—Humor.   1. Title.   II. Series:
Boyd, Jack, 1932–   Cedar Gap archives : v. 2.
F391.2.B67   1990
976.4—dc20   90-33521
                                                              CIP

Texas Tech University Press
Lubbock, Texas 79409-1037 USA

PREFACE

ou seldom see anybody wearing a classic of
that rarity. The danger is too great. You
play a classic on your record player, say,
Elvis on an early Sun 45, and you lovingly
sponge off the dust. Don't you always park
your classic '32 Hispano-Suiza in your garage under a felt-lined tarp? Of course, you
do. You take care of classics.

You don't wear a classic, at least not in West Texas.

But this guy was wearing a certifiable classic. You could get pedi-
gree papers on it.

My hamburger was so-so, so I spent much of my time averting my
eyes from its greasy onions and watery mustard. My migratory gaze
fell on a stocky, middle-aged man just as he noisily scooted back his
chair and homed in on my booth, frowning all the way. He slid in
beside me.

"You the guy that writes that Cedar Gap thing?"

I pointed at my mouth as if I'd just taken a bite and then swigged
some iced tea. That gave me a few seconds to size up a man who
would wear a classic 1968 lime-green polyester leisure suit with orange piping to a hamburger joint. I mean, you could spill catsup or

Co'Cola on such a classic, and in a trice—we're talking an extremely *short* trice—totally destroy something that could never be replaced. A man so lacking in judgment could easily be a serial murderer.

"Well, *are* ya?"

"Uh, yeah," I said. Fortunately, I'm at my voluble best under such pressure. The words just pour out.

"Why'dja change their names?"

I'd expected several other phrases. "Like your stories" came to mind. Or, "I got this great yarn about my dog you oughta hear." Or, "I'll be shootin' ya now." But definitely not something about name changes.

"What?" I said. The glib Silver Tongue of the Brazos flapped on.

"Listen, I know personally ever' one a those people you been writin' about down there in Cedar Gap, an' I just gotta know why you changed all a their names."

"Well, actually . . ."

"It's them lawyers, ain't it?"

"Well, actually . . ."

"It's OK, I can hold a secret."

"Well, actually . . ."

"I knew it!" He winked broadly. "Tell ya what. You just keep on with them made-up names, and only me an' you'll know the real truth." He grunted as he pushed himself out of the narrow booth.

Since it appeared I would survive to finish my lackluster meal, as a reward I gave him my best John Le Carré conspiratorial smirk. He frowned and squinted, not quite understanding. I saw I had to say something positive.

"Like your suit."

"Like your stories." He winked and swaggered back to his chicken-fried steak.

There's a sermon lurking in there somewhere.

CONTENTS

*This one's for
Rebecca and Glenn,
who believed*

Boy,
Howdy!

CEDAR GAP ARCHIVES
Vera Frudenberg and Luther Gravely
Archivists and series editors

The Volumes

Life As It's Lived
Boy, Howdy!

CHAPTER 1

COUPLES

Truman and Wanda: Newlyweds

The brawn of a community is its couples. There are, of course, a bunch of folks who, because of a rational decision, lack of motivation or pure sorry luck, have wound up flying their mortal coil solo. And for the most part, these singles do valuable work. But the bulk of a community's traditions and tax revenues come from the pairs of former individuals who have "found each other." Thus, in this opera plot called life, Cedar Gap duets outnumber Cedar Gap soloists by a considerable stretch.

And they seem to stay together. Whether that's because of innate fidelity or latent sloth no one has determined. My own theory is that, in several cases, each member of the pair is so bewildered by the other's obscure reasoning and total lack of comprehension that they stay together just to see what's going to go wrong next. Or maybe they figure all remaining members of the opposite sex have the same mystifying habits, so they may as well stay in familiar, if befuddling, territory. Sort of, the devil you know.

Possibly that's too harsh a judgment. We all know couples who go around in a state of thinly disguised euphoria simply because each thinks that he or she has been chosen or thought far enough ahead to do the choosing. That was the case with Wanda and Truman Roe.

Truman runs a bread route out of Abilene. About a year ago it dawned on him that eating a cold supper by himself wasn't all that wonderful. As he said, "New baked bread smells nice, but it lacks a lot when compared to a freshly scrubbed and starched lady."

That was about the time he noticed Wanda, although just why he noticed her remains unclear.

Wanda was the unclaimed jewel in Mayor Yancy McWhirter's family. Like Truman, she's in her mid-thirties, but unlike Truman, she didn't smile a lot. Wanda quit smiling when the Big Three-O rolled around without a man to help her count.

The problem has been Wanda's attitude.

"I just don't understand my daughter," Yancy complained. "Her clothes are a mess, she won't wear makeup. You've seen that plain-Jane hairdo, and she can't cook worth a flip. She's just flat given up." He looked around for community reinforcement. "When I say something to her, she just sneers that 'Tom Selleck would be fine, if he'll take me like I am.'"

Six months ago, Truman sat nursing a cup of Palace Cafe coffee when Wanda slouched in for a newspaper. Truman kept his back turned, but in a voice just loud enough to carry he muttered, "I tell you, that woman must have studied ballet all her life. She carries herself better than anybody in town."

Wanda glanced around carefully. Outside of IdaLou Vanderburg, our sixty-five-year-old cafe cook, and Tootles the cat, she was the only female in the place. Wanda's back straightened and she glided out without turning.

The next week Truman happened into Oliver Greenslope's Drugstore at the same time as Wanda. "Oliver, you remember that cornbread we had at the last church picnic? I sure need to find out who baked that. I took some to our head baker, and he said anybody who could make something fall that gracefully has got to be a pure genius."

The whole town knows cornbread is the only thing Wanda can fix without totally destroying it. She pretended she didn't hear Truman, but at the next church picnic her cornbread was flanked by some reasonably acceptable raisin rolls and a pan of what several people recognized as cupcakes.

Truman spread several more indirect compliments before asking Wanda to drive with him to a ball game down at Winters. His flattery was never actually mentioned, but Wanda sat very straight, her hands moved like cobwebs in a breeze, and the basket of snacking goodies she brought flavored the entire bleacher section.

When Truman brought her home he nodded shyly. "Wanda, please excuse me for sayin' this, but"—he paused in speechless admiration—"you must read every style book in the country. I just gotta tell you, those little ringlets on your neck are as classy a thing as I've ever seen around here."

She never let on that her bun had merely slipped a few sprouts. But from then on she got up an hour early to twist ringlets to match the lace collar on her new Butterick frock.

They never actually got around to deciding to get married. Truman merely let it slip at the cafe that he'd ordered a complete state-of-the-art kitchen from Houston because "anything less would be an insult to such a natural homemaker as Wanda. I mean, you just can't insult an artist by giving her cheap tools."

By this time Wanda was buying her clothes in Fort Worth, Corinne Iverson over at the Fountainebleau Beauty Spa was doing Wanda's hair every week, and Yancy was wondering when they could cut out that *cordon bleu* stuff and get back to chicken-fried steak.

The wedding was set for a Sunday afternoon in the house Truman bought and renovated. Wanda stood smiling like some Greek statue. Truman blew a major chunk of cash on the flowers he had flown in from California and the string quartet he imported from San Antonio. Somebody chided him for his overindulgence.

"Look," he said in a stage whisper, "if the Queen of England came for a visit, would you pick some daisies from a bar ditch and turn up a tape of Johnny Cash? 'Course not. If you're marrying into royalty, you deal with them like royalty."

They got back on Wednesday, and ever since then Wanda has

treated Truman as some sort of minor deity. As Wanda said, "If he likes ringlets, he gets ringlets, because the man obviously has impeccable taste."

And Truman? He just sits around and smiles a lot.

For Better 'r Worse, Sick 'r Healthy, I Reckon I Do

Truman and Wanda will make it if only because, during any given instant, at least one of them knows what's going on. With Vern and Lou Ella Gilzinski, however, you can make book that things are going to get a tad thorny. If, as they say, the course of true love seldom runs smooth, then the Ordwill-Gilzinski marriage is destined to be the Snake River rapids of marital streams.

Any couple married more than an hour will testify that just a smidgin of dislike adds a certain spice to a relationship. She can't stand his glimmer-eyed racing to get through a stoplight and save four seconds. Contrarily, he can't understand her total oblivion to the fact that nobody truly cares if her shoes don't match the hood ornament when she picks up the kids at school.

But Lou Ella and Vern were light years beyond mere dislike or a tiny fit of pique. They've known and hated each other since third grade when he glued shut all of the pages of her Tiny Tots Sunday School Hymnal and she emptied a bottle of constipation remedy in his dog's dish.

With that sort of wretched loathing as a foundation, it was only natural they should, as high school seniors, decide marriage was the next logical step.

Lou Ella Ordwill and Vernon Gilzinski graduated last May. They postponed the wedding this long so he could get a job and she could train him properly. While that was never actually stated in such bald language, Lou Ella's agenda was definitely in place.

"Isn't the Pierced Royal Hungarian flatware just perfect?" Lou Ella said.

"I don't want any spoons I can see through," Vern said. "Just make it like what my mama's always used."

Lou Ella frowned and tilted her head. She worked the phrase "*my mama*" around in her mouth several times before she said, quite slowly, "Your mama's taste is, ummmmm, sort of old-fashioned."

"'You sayin' my mama hasn't got good taste?"

"No, Vernon, Sweetie, I just want something more, ah, stylish."

Vern's jaw muscles bunched nervously. "Like those invitations that remind me of the curtains down in the funeral parlor?"

Unfortunately, weddings always have several drivers, a problem akin to feeding No-Doz to a double team of Clydesdales. Mrs. Gilzinski and Mrs. Ordwill, backing their offspring to perdition and back, pasted on glazed smiles and suggested diametrically opposed ways of furthering a ceremony already thickly larded with traditional silliness.

"Honey," Mrs. Ordwill said smoothly, "you remember we've already talked about having my darling nephew, Roy Willie, carry the ring. Wouldn't my sister's boy be just perfect?"

The word *perfect* is seldom used in the vicinity of Roy Willie. He's just under five years old, not quite potty trained, and sports the vocabulary of a hemorrhoidal stevedore. Mrs. Gilzinski blanched at the thought of such a primate lurching along next to her own delicate niece, Missy Beth, who had better be the flower girl. But she held her peace; decorations were next on the list, and the up-state votes were needed.

"Now," Mrs. Gilzinski oozed, "I've got some zinnias in my collection that would be delightful on the pulpit area. We could . . ."

"What color are they?" Mrs. Ordwill asked, her tone indicating there were insurmountable problems with the zinnias no matter what their color.

Mrs. Gilzinski swiveled her head, her smile halfway between Betty Crocker and Attila the Hun. "A perfect sunset orange."

"Oh," Mrs. Ordwill said, shrugging, "I'm afraid that would never do. It would clash with the bridesmaid's yellow sashes."

"Naw, orange would be just fine," Vern said, oblivious as usual to the world and its problems. "We're gonna have the wedding outside in our yard, and anything would look OK there." He took a step back as the sound of three women grinding their teeth echoed through the funereal gloom.

The final abrasive clash came at the wedding rehearsal that Thursday night. The organist at the First Baptist Church presented her own list of wedding music, which consisted entirely of songs popular when Teddy Roosevelt was president.

"Oh, no," Lou Ella groaned. "We've got to have love songs by Carly Simon and James Taylor or I'll just die. I mean, really, *really* die."

Vernon, his Lone Star viciousness a product of having moved to Texas at age six, stated flatly, "I don't think so. I figured on usin' some Willie an' Merle, an' maybe an old instrumental by Bob Wills for the processional."

Right after the wedding Lou Ella and Vernon left for a long weekend in San Antonio. Lou Ella hunched over on her side of the car celebrating her Simon/Taylor music and bemoaning sashes changed to orange, while Vernon sat in a confused meditation on certain qualities in his bride he had never before considered, like greed, hysteria, and having a mother.

Everybody in town agrees that it was a perfect wedding, just like all the rest.

Finus's Ol' Quarter Section

With some couples it seems that, no matter what happens, there's still the two of them. Even if one of them passes on, it's not like that one died, but merely stepped around the corner. The glow is still a two-part glow. Amy and Finus Greeley formed that sort of team.

We think about Amy and Finus just about every Saturday when Amy Greeley leans back in the Palace Cafe, raises her coffee cup, and mumbles something. We never quite catch what she says before she replaces her cup.

Even in her seventies, Amy is still gorgeous. Back in the thirties, Amethyst White was Taylor County's raging beauty. Ripe wheat hair sparkled around periwinkle eyes and a perfect face. Every male between twelve and ninety built hours of idolatrous daydreams around Amy's slim, graceful figure and her honey-smooth alto voice.

That spring of 1934 there must have been a dozen money pools bet on which oilman or cattle baron she would finally choose.

Nobody won a single pool because Amy White choose to marry beneath her gifts. It wasn't a dark horse that won; Finus Greeley couldn't even come up to horse. In the eyes of Cedar Gap, Finus was more on the order of a plowing mule.

There was nothing really wrong with Finus. He was just plain. "You could splash him with red paint," the mayor of Cedar Gap snorted, "and he still wouldn't stand out in a crowd of three people." True, his old '25 A-Model Ford was paid off and ran perfectly, but it was far beneath the Buicks and Pierce-Arrows and the single Duesenburg sported by the rest of Amy's suitors.

And as for land, Finus Greeley was a relative pauper: 160 acres. Even Finus didn't think much of it, calling it "that ol' quarter section of mine."

"Well, it ain't all that bad a piece a proppity," Mort Watkins mumbled. "He's got a good spring-fed creek, an' there's always deer, an' there's hunnurts a squirrels in those wild pecan trees in his bottomland." Mort spread his hands helplessly. "But . . . , it's only a quarter section!"

Finus went to church regularly, doffed his hat and said, "Yes, ma'am," to every woman he met, and was never known to go back on his word. But still, he only owned that spindly quarter section.

Here was a beautiful, bright woman who could have married any man within a day's drive. Instead, she chose a muddle-faced, quiet farmer—you can't be a rancher with 160 acres!—living in a four-room house on a quarter section. Besides having a face as plain as a caliche road, Finus was shorter than Amy by two inches. We thought we were going to have to have her mama committed, Mrs. White was so agitated.

Cedar Gap never really got used to seeing Finus and Amy walking around quietly, laughing at private jokes, bending over coffee in the Palace Cafe. What hurt them the worst was that Amy seemed to be enjoying her privations.

Amy never let on that she'd married beneath her station. She smiled as she fixed up the four-room house. When a boy and then a girl came along Finus paid cash for some lumber, then single-handedly built a three-room addition. He worked long hours, fixed everything he owned, rebuilt a used tractor, and improved his bottomland.

That summer of '37 people finally started paying attention to that bottomland Finus worked. With crops burning up everywhere in the county, Finus paid cash for a pump and sprayer and pumped water from his creek onto his wheat field. He ran cattle and still had plenty of hay to last him through the winter. He also made enough money to buy a used '34 Pontiac. As always, he paid cash. But Amy deserved better.

That was the same year Amy's suitor with the Buick lost all his money in some oil speculation. The next year, another former pursuer went to jail for stock fraud. In '42, the rich Duesenburg owner deteriorated until he went crazy and then shot himself. People shook their heads and frowned and wondered how Amy made such a lucky guess.

Naturally, Finus never got elected to the Farm Bureau or the school board. A short, plain man with a measly quarter section who took the only truly world-class woman in Cedar Gap's history out of circulation shouldn't even hope to be popular. Boy, howdy! Old lust remembers.

Finus was killed in a nameless jungle in New Guinea two weeks before World War II ended. His kids were seven and five.

That was when Cedar Gap realized why Amy White married plain, short, uninspiring Finus Greeley. He had developed his bottomland until it was so rich you could grow anything on it in any season, dry or wet. His small select herd of cattle produced bulls selling for unheard of prices. And the oil rights Finus had reserved when everyone else was selling out made Amy and the kids secure for life.

When Amy Greeley finishes her trading here in town, she'll talk awhile in the Palace Cafe, and then say something like, "Well, I better be getting back to Finus's ol' quarter section." But before she leaves she always lifts her coffee cup and mumbles a few words, as if toasting somebody or something.

We're not sure what she's thinking or what she says, but her eyes blur a little and she always smiles when she does it.

Travels with Duke 'n Bunny

You open a book like this one and, although there's a left page and a right page, they form a continuous story. Couples generally follow such a chapter form in that conversations and ideas alternate and occasionally even deviate. But they always have some nodding acquaintance with the same story.

Duke and Bunny McKirkle haven't lived in the same story for decades. It's not that they don't love each other. They truly do. But if their history is ever published, Bunny's love story will be serialized in *Amazing Romances* while Duke's will be a lecture series in a Rand-McNally atlas.

And just now they walked out to start their vacation.

They've only been planning their vacation for two months, but given the variables it seems like a year. As with many couples, it's not where you go, it's how you describe getting there.

"Where y'all headin' out for, Duke?" somebody in the Palace Cafe asked innocently, totally disregarding Duke's cartographic history.

"We're gonna ease up to the Interstate an' nudge west over through Sweetwater and then north at Roscoe, although that construction around Sweetwater can be a problem, so we might head north just the other side a Merkel, you know, through Sylvester an' then cut over on 180 to come out at Snyder." Commas figure much higher than periods on Duke's personal list of breathing spaces.

"Duke," Bunny said placidly, "I think they mean *where* are we going?"

"Well, you cain't disregard the roads," Duke said. "That's part of the 'where.' I mean, we're goin' through Lubbock eventually, but we may go up to Anson an' turn west across 180, which would get us to Roby about the same time as goin' through Merkel and Sylvester."

Bunny rolled her eyes. "We're going to that nice resort up near Sante Fe. Duke?" She turned and frowned sweetly. "Isn't that in Colorado or someplace out there?"

Duke blinked. "New Mexico," he said impatiently. "Santa Fe's in New Mexico. You remember we went out through Lamesa and Hobbs that time and cut into State Road 18 to get to Roswell, then we went up through Vaughn and Cline's Corners on U.S. 285. Then we had the choice of bendin' west through . . ."

She cut him off with a wave of her hand. "I remember! That was the time we ate at that Dairy Queen with that real clean ladies room, then we backtracked to the nice man selling Pecos canteloupe and we turned"—she pointed with her coffee cup—"that way."

"West. When you're goin' south a right turn gets you goin' west." He sighed. "We turned west on 180 at Snyder. We shoulda gone on up to Post and turned on 380 so we could go through Tahoka, but . . ."

"Whatever. I remember finishing that article on quilts in *Texas Highways*, and just then we passed that adobe Texaco station where the Methodist kids were washing cars to take a missionary trip to South Dakota or somewhere."

Duke shook his head sadly. "That was Hobbs. It was 132 miles from Snyder to Hobbs on U.S. 180. We probably shoulda gone on over through Artesia on U.S. 82, and from there . . ."

"Duke," Bunny said softly, "stuff a sock in it. Nobody truly cares about how far it is to wherever it was you were blabbering about."

"Yeah! Right!" Duke banged his cup on the table for emphasis. "You start out that 41 miles from Lamesa to Seminole with less 'n a quarter tank a gas, and then you'll care how far it is."

Bunny patted her husband's thick, calloused hand. "All I want to do is go by that little stand that sold hankies made out of cactus where we turned and went into the setting sun. You remember how bright that sun was, don't you? You got so mad!" She giggled lightly.

"That was I-40, and we turned west. The sun sets in the west, you know. Has for a long time."

"Whatever. We turned right after that real nice shopping center and followed the mountains, but we stopped for some silver jewelry and saw that darlin' little Indian baby. You remember! He smiled at you, and you acted real silly like the baby knew you, or something."

"Sure, that was on I-25, maybe sixteen, eighteen miles above Albuquerque."

"Really? Did we go through Albuquerque?"

"We *always* go through Albuquerque if we wanta stay on the Interstate." They got up to leave. "'Course, this time we could go straight on up 285 to cut into I-25 near Glorietta." They walked out hand in hand.

"Isn't that where we got those beautiful postcards from that nice couple, and he had a glass eye?"

"I dunno. I just know it's a two-lane road with nary a curve in forty-eight miles, which is my kind a road. Ya know, instead of hittin' Cline's Corners we might take 84 up through Santa Rosa, and then over on I-40 to . . ."

Their voices drifted away as Bunny waved good-bye. Now all we have to worry about is the slide show when they get back.

SATURDAY'S JOURNAL

ME 'N THE BOY PREFER

IT THAT WAY

ell, it's kind of awkward here in Cedar Gap today. For most people it's just another Saturday, but for Wyatt Blynn, the last twenty-four hours have been a mountain-top turning point.

Wyatt and Edith Blynn give new meaning to the word *grooved*. As he's said weekly, "There's a right way and a wrong way to plow, and me 'n the boy just seem to prefer the right way." Substitute tightening fences or roofing sheds or getting his hair cut for the word *plow* and you get identical concepts. The idea is to get it right, and then keep it there.

Edith, through no fault of her own, has a limited cooking repertoire. The fourth night of their marriage she fixed a tuna casserole. Wyatt sat his coffee carefully just above his knife, and then said, "Those were good pork chops last Monday. Reckon we could plan on those, say, Mondays and Thursdays?"

From then on, it was pork chops, fried chicken and steak on a three-day rotation, with roast beef every Sunday. The only break came with a gala Friday evening out—it was always Friday—at the Palace Cafe.

Every time it was the same. "Edith, why don't we take this table by the window. Good view without a draft."

The waitress always handed them two menus, which for at least three decades has contained exactly the same six possibilities. Still, every time Wyatt perused the menu like Dewey rereading the election returns.

"Edith, how does the chili sound to you?" The fact that for twelve consecutive years Edith had ordered the chili with saltines and iced tea seemingly made no impression on Wyatt. "And . . . I guess, oh, I'll . . . ah . . . I'll have the barbecue. Let's see, what comes with that? Oh, here it is. I'll have the baked beans and . . . the . . . potato salad." He'd slap the menu shut, satisfied with his decisions. Exactly the same decisions he'd made every Friday night for twelve years.

Nothing changed when Dwayne and Vicki were born. The menu stayed precisely the same and so did the Blynn choices.

Finally, about ten years ago, Dwayne hit the first grade. Wyatt proudly asked for separate menus for the menfolk, and then turned ceremoniously to the heir of the mortgage. "And what looks good to you, Dwayne?"

The six-year-old boy scanned the menu, but all he'd ever heard was the trio of basics from his father. "Uh, . . . oh, I'll have the barbecue, and the baked beans, and . . . the . . . potato salad." The rhythm and inflection were exact duplicates of his father's. Dwayne slapped the menu shut and handed it proudly to his beaming daddy. The next year Vicki slipped easily into the chili/saltines habit.

Tradition. Continuity. Death, taxes, and Wyatt Blynn's family diet. Things you can count on.

Then, last night the four of them walked in and got their accustomed table by the window. Everyone did a sing-along as Wyatt ordered for himself and Edith. Then, "What looks good to you, Dwayne?"

Dwayne, a rail-thin sixteen-year-old two inches taller than his daddy, hesitated just one beat longer than normal. Several people felt the rhythm change and gagged on their iced tea. The whole room quieted.

"Aw, I don't know, Dad. I think . . . the chicken-fried steak sounds pretty good tonight." Heads swivelled, jaws dropped. "And, tell ya what, Miss Kollwood, how about some creamed corn, fried okra, and maybe an extra bowl of gravy." He looked up, completely unaware of civilization's mutation.

Stunned, Wyatt leaned back in his chair. He slowly reopened his own menu to check if those particular foods were, in fact, available anywhere near Cedar Gap. Yeah, there they were. He frowned and nodded.

Edith swallowed and looked back at her own menu. "Brenda Beth," she said in a tight-throated whisper, "how about canceling that order of chili. I think I'll have the chef's salad . . . and a Coke."

Vicki's wide-eyed gaze ricocheted around the table. "OK, then I want a cheeseburger and a Dr Pepper." She smiled broadly at her father. "Wow, this is the best meal we've ever had, isn't it, Dad?"

It could have been had not Wyatt been in an open-eyed coma. He slowly handed the unslammed menu back to Brenda Beth, who, sensing the historic quality of the night, backed up slowly and walked through the tomblike silence to the kitchen.

That was last night. Saturdays, Wyatt always visited, in order, the Feed & Lumber, the Cedar Gap Mercantile and finally the Palace Cafe for exactly two cups of coffee.

But today he started at the cafe. All he could do was shake his head and stir his coffee. Finally he got up and angled out the door.

"Leavin' so soon, Wyatt?" somebody said.

"Yeah. I gotta check on a new kind of claw hammer I heard somebody mention last week. Might be an . . . improvement on what I've been usin'."

Like they say, when the dam breaks, the valley's never the same.

CHAPTER 2

THE NOBLE WOMEN

OF CEDAR GAP

Sylvia's Group Insurance Plan

our average man has a feeling that there is no such thing as an average woman. Part of that conundrum has to do with the Female Inverse Ratio Law, which is a sub-codicil of Mrs. Murphy's Law. The FIR Law states: "The less important the decision, the more time it takes. And the reverse."

Stafford Higginbotham shook his head as he described his Aunt Totie when she was trying to decide on the color of some buttons for her new spring frock.

"Aunt Totie wasted a full afternoon stewin' about those fool buttons. In three hours she cried twice, insulted four friends, and alienated the entire Cedar Gap Floral Artistry Club. Just as she was about to trash the whole idea, Cutter, her two-year-old, got half a Vienna sausage lodged in his throat.

"You'd have to measure her movements in microseconds as she snatched Cutter off the floor, held him upside down with one hand, and with the other hand gave him a karate chop that shot the half-chewed Vienna sausage clear through the open window. Without breaking stride, she went back to worrying the button idea like a hound worrying a bone."

Of course, not all of the women of Cedar Gap use native intuition to solve important problems. Sometimes it's just pure, hard, clench-jawed reasoning. Those hard decisions came to mind sometime back when we waved Sylvia Froberger back into town. We'd waited a bunch of years for the privilege, and it felt good.

Fourteen years ago Guy Froberger died in a car wreck on the way home from his job in the oil patch. At that time oil money was coming in pretty good, but with four growing kids Sylvia and Guy still stood with their backs pretty close to the wall. Guy's death left Sylvia with Bennie, Dawn, Robert and Sandy, and not much else.

One blustery, cold December day during Bennie's senior year in high school, Sylvia called a family meeting. "You're all going to college," she said carefully.

Bennie shrugged. "Maybe someday, but the day I graduate from high school I'm gettin' a job on a rig."

"You," Sylvia said, nodding toward her oldest, "can get whatever job you please when you graduate, but come September you'll be in college somewhere. Start applying." She turned to the other three. "As for the rest of us, we'll help Bennie. And when Bennie graduates, he'll help you three until everybody graduates."

Robert, his adolescent belligerence developing daily, folded his arms. "Naw, sir, there ain't no way I'm helpin' Bennie. He's made fun of me and thumped my head too many times. The only thing he'll get from me is a wave outa town."

The steely glint to Sylvia's voice caught all of the kids by surprise. "No, you're wrong, Robert. Bennie will work at school for his room and board, and you and Dawn and Sandy and I will work to pay for his tuition and books. If Bennie can make enough this summer to get an old car, then he rides. If not, he walks." Her voice dropped to a whisper. "But we *will* help Bennie through college." She gazed deeply in her oldest son's eyes. "And when he graduates, he *will* help the rest of you."

No doubt that same tone of voice came out when Moses called over his shoulder, "I think we'll be leaving now, Pharaoh." It left no room for argumentative maneuvering. The children sat like sticks of stovewood as Sylvia outlined the next twelve years of their lives.

"You'll all get jobs, and half of what you make goes into the college fund. Then, you'll get your turn when you get in college."

"Now, just a darn minute!" Dawn said. Her mother's head snapped around so fast it created a breeze. "I mean, just a minute. I've gotta have a new dress for the high school dance."

"If it can come out of your half of the money you make, then you'll have no problem. You may have to do more than babysit."

Sandy, the youngest, smirked. "I'm too little. I don't have to . . ."

Sylvia tilted her head toward her nine-year-old. "There are pecans all over this town that are never harvested. You'll gather those, and you'll rake leaves and grow tomatoes, and everybody will take care of this house while I get a second job."

And that's the way it worked for what came to be known as Mama's Group Insurance Plan. Every vacation Bennie roughnecked for an oil rig. Through the years Dawn washed dishes at the Palace Cafe, Robert carried two paper routes, and Sandy peddled her shelled pecans.

Four years later Bennie graduated with honors, and then got a good accounting job in Dallas. Every month he sent money back while Dawn, Robert, and finally Sandy, worked their way through college.

One bright spring morning just before Sandy's graduation the college got wind of Sylvia's long-range family project. The administration contacted Bennie to ask him what he thought of a certain idea.

When he finally got his breath, Bennie said, "It's perfect."

Sandy graduated with honors, the fourth Froberger kid to do so. Robert and Bennie sat proudly in the audience while Dawn prepared to hood Sandy.

Sylvia would have performed the hooding ceremony as she had with the other three, but she was taking care of some official duties. Just before the hooding, the president of the college arose to read a proclamation granting Sylvia Froberger an honorary bachelor's degree. "Plus," he said, "we have asked her to fill a temporary one-day position as Professor of Studies in the American Way."

He helped Sylvia into a black robe. Then, to thunderous applause, he led her to a reserved seat among the school's faculty. She sat primly erect, holding a small engraved plaque. Her gaze never left her four children.

And their gaze never left her.

Dieting with the Natives

America seems to feel that the more money you make, the skinnier you should look. That may explain Cedar Gap's jaundiced view of dieting as a life-style. What it does *not* explain is that time a while back when we actually listened to some of Dolly Hooter's advice. As a group, this town achieved its goal of losing just over a quarter ton of blubber. It also created more stress than a Communist on the school board. However, the biggest surprise came at the final weigh-in.

Three months ago Dolly Hooter, our intrepid reporter for the *Cedar Gap Galaxy-Telegraph*, received a letter addressed to her bi-weekly advice column, "Talk to Me!" That letter focused her restless search for a citywide crusade.

The upshot was Cedar Gap's First Annual Weight Loss Olympics. Since getting in the heads of the cellulite-laden citizenry was the first shot of the Battle of the Chubs, Dolly contacted Luther "20-20" Gravely, our area inebriate and chief mind-bender.

"Luther," Dolly said, shaking the spongelike form. "Wake up. We're organizing a diet plan for Cedar Gap."

Luther squinted until both eyes focused on the same spitcurl. "We? Is this a sizable group, or is all of 'we' right here?"

"We're just the beginning. If we lead, hundreds will follow."

Luther felt around for someplace to stand up, but everything was already occupied either by air or sunlight, neither of which would help his megaton headache. He stayed hunched over, his head in his hands. "Dolly, help me out here. Just why are we doing this?"

"It's for their own good."

"Seems to me Hitler used that phrase a lot."

Dolly ignored the slurred remark. "What's the first thing we gotta do to make people want to lose weight?"

"Pay 'em money. Pay 'em a *lot* of money."

"Haven't got any money. What's next?"

Luther rubbed his stubble-covered jaw. "Embarrassment hasn't worked too well with this bunch. Maybe civic pride could do it."

"*That's it!*" Dolly shouted as Luther fainted at the noise. "Beautify Cedar Gap! Lose those pounds!"

The result was an entire front page of the *Galaxy-Telegraph* devoted to corpulence and gluttony. The headline, UGLY FAT KILLING CEDAR GAP, used the same size type as JAPS BOMB PEARL HARBOR.

The text was vintage Hooter: "Lard. Look up the word. It's the fat of a pig. Does that describe you?" Dolly wasn't angry, she was just cutting through the standard *Galaxy-Telegraph* mush of wedding announcements, cattle sales, and wild grape jam recipes.

Over thirty people signed on for the three-month program, the goal being to lose an aggregate quarter ton of fat. Unfortunately, some were better candidates than others. Elmore "No-Neck" Noonan, who at six-six casts a shadow like a field-dressed rhino, bent over Dolly's sign-up sheet at a card table in the Palace Cafe. "I'm good for a couple of pounds, Miss Hooter."

Somebody muttered, "The only way No-Neck'll lose two pounds is if we cut off his big toe."

Wilson Kruddmeier, our district auditor, was told in nonambiguous terms to weigh in everybody, keep his mouth shut about beginning and ending weights, and only release the net loss.

The excuses and pleas for exemptions were inventive and unending.

"Wait a minute. I'm wearin' my contact lenses, so we better cut at least a pound off'n whatever that scale says."

"Listen, Wilson, I'm gettin' a haircut. Can ya figure that against my total?"

It's been a thorny process, but everybody managed four ounces here, half a pound there, down to the final two weeks. The only exception was Bertie Faye Hogg, our prophetically named postmistress. She not only didn't lose, she put on three pounds, to the consternation of the Loser's League.

But two weeks ago Bertie Faye disappeared. "She said somethin' about seein' an aunt down in Brownsville," her substitute said.

Then, about an hour before the end of the contest, a dramatically slimmed down Bertie Faye waltzed in the Palace Cafe wearing a skin-tight dress from Nieman's. The crowd sucked in its breath as she stepped daintily onto the scale. Wilson peered at the scale, then at his notebook. "Thirty pounds!" he shouted.

"Bertie Faye!" somebody yelled. "You look great!

Great, of course, is a comparative word in the case of Bertie Faye Hogg. Going from 180 to 150 is obvious but not earth-shaking. Still, it's a loss, and it put the town over the top, lard-wise.

Bertie Faye's little Mona Lisa smile never wavered as people plied her with questions about her secret. "Betcha went to one of those expensive spas over in Dallas." "Now, don't tell us you used one of those fat suckers we been readin' about." "Come on, Bertie Faye, how'd you do it?"

Finally, Bertie Faye laughed. "Actually, it was fairly easy. I just went down to South Texas, waltzed across the border, and checked into a hotel in Nuevo Laredo. Then I drank three full glasses of their water. About twenty-four hours later, I started losing weight. A lot of weight. An *awful* lot of weight." She turned and did a galumph-ing pirouette. "It's not the best way, but it worked!"

Several people blanched as the cafe went dead silent. Wilson Krudd-meier snapped his notebook shut. The Lardy Olympics were over.

Donnie Sue, the Celebrated Legend of Boston

Donnie Sue just got back from her week in Boston. She left here a local phenomenon and returned a Yankee legend. What bought her that place in Northeastern folklore was not a cool, slow, reasoned response to opportunity, but that lightning bolt of intuition for which she and other Cedar Gap women are famous.

Deputy Sheriff Donnie Sue Kingsbury read about a short course in electronic surveillance put on in Boston by the F.B.I. Donnie Sue, who's been called Dirty Harry with an attitude problem, figured electronic surveillance might give her an alternative to some of her nontraditional law enforcement techniques, the ones that cause the most pain to lawbreakers.

"Hey, Donnie Sue," somebody called across the Palace Cafe, "you takin' that chrome-plated howitzer of yours on the plane?"

"No need," she said, patting her .44 magnum with the seven-inch barrel. "When I leave Texas I'm just a civilian."

Everybody grinned as she left. Murphy Gumpton sipped his coffee. "Reckon I oughta call ahead," he asked, "and warn them Yankees?" Everybody thought about it for a second, and then they frowned and shook their heads. "You're probably right," Murph said. "Let's just let Donnie Sue surprise 'em!"

Donnie Sue arrived in Boston late at night. She would have choked on the eighteen-dollar ride to the convention center if the cab hadn't screeched to a stop in front of a police barricade.

"Park it, fella," a hassled cop snarled. "We got a hostage situation here."

Donnie Sue leapt from the cab as she clawed through her purse for her identification and shield. "Hey, Sheriff, who's bein' held?"

The policeman's gaze zigzagged from the shield to the short, bright-eyed blonde. "Just stay behind the barrier, Sister. A guy's got two little girls in that store over there, and we're waitin' to see what . . ."

"A guy? ONE GUY?" Donnie Sue's face twisted into a scowling fist. "You only got one jerk scarin' two precious little girls?" She stuck her face six inches from the policeman's startled eyes. "What're ya gonna do?"

"Well, uh," the policeman backpedaled, "we got a standud wait-and-see policy for . . ."

"Wait? For what? For the jerk to get enough guts to do somethin' truly dumb, like shootin' his way out holdin' one of those little girls?"

"You don't undastand, Sister. Policy states . . ."

"I cain't believe this!" Donnie Sue shoved the startled cabbie aside as she yanked his cab door open. "I heard somethin' rattle when ya turned that last corner . . . there it is!" She grabbed a two-foot length of lead pipe partially wrapped with tape. "Ooooo! Nice!"

She shoved the lead pipe up her right sleeve as she sprinted toward a dark nearby alley. She kicked over three garbage cans till she found what she wanted; a used pizza box. Then she edged around to the front of the store where the hostages were held.

With the box held high in her left hand, she kicked on the door and yelled, "Pizza! Aw'right, who ordered this pizza?"

Every sound on the street ceased. The police stood open-mouthed. There was no sound from the storefront. "I said, '*Who ordered this pizza?*' Either come get it, or I'm takin' it . . ."

The door opened to a slit. "Ain't nobody in here ordered no pizza!"

Donnie Sue squinted up at the storefront. "Yeah? Well, this is Frank's Tie Shop, so this is Frank's pizza." She heard two tiny voices snuffling in the background. "Somebody's already paid for this pizza, so do you want it, or do I pop this beer and eat it myself?"

There was no sound. Then, slowly, the door opened and a hand reached for the pizza box. Donnie Sue turned her head slightly and faked a sneeze, pulling the box farther away from the door. The hand reached for the waving box. Suddenly Donnie Sue grabbed the reaching hand and yanked as she dropped her own right arm. The lead pipe was a blur as it slid into her hand and then whipped around to catch the man diagonally across his nose and jaw.

As she said later, "It sounded just like steppin' on one of those little wooden strawberry baskets."

In the five seconds it took the policemen to reach her, she stomped the man's gun hand, broke both his kneecaps, and grabbed the two little girls in a bear hug.

As Donnie Sue explained over the phone, "That jerk lost a whole lot of enthusiasm at about the same time he lost most of his teeth and a major portion of lip." She hesitated. "I only got chewed out by three officials before I began tapping the lead pipe against my knee. Then they sorta got a greater appreciation of the problem."

Like I say, Donnie Sue is now a Boston legend. Of course, those folks are hard up for legends. Here in Cedar Gap, we seem to have one on about every corner.

SATURDAY'S JOURNAL

UNCLE MILO'S GIRLFRIEND,

BY TURNBOW SHIVELY

ell, it's a pretty good Saturday here in Cedar Gap, Mrs. Orabone, even if we gotta write some of that streamy-conscience stuff for your English class about things that just sorta happened. You said you truly hated that kinda writing, but we should try some of it so we'd know why it was worthless. So, OK, here goes.

This story of mine started a couple of days ago when Uncle Milo was sitting around talking about how dangerous flying is. My uncle Milo Shively is the crop duster here in Cedar Gap, and he said it was probably best that only men did the flying because women tend to be too flighty—that was his word—for real flying. That got a big laugh from everybody except the women, which included Miss Sue Etta Bruff.

"Milo Shively," she said. "I've been to Dallas and Austin both in a plane." Miss Sue Etta Bruff is real old, about twenty-six or forty or something up there. "So you can just take back that mail shovin'-ism." I ain't too sure what that is, but if the mailman delivers it, it cain't be real bad.

The upshot was Uncle Milo challenged her to a thirty-minute

flight. His old biplane is really a single-seater, but he's got a little place behind the seat where somebody can sit if they aren't too particular about being cramped or about sitting on an old hay baler seat he welded onto the plane's frame.

Actually, I think it was a trick to get off by theirselves. Uncle Milo'd bought Miss Sue Etta four or five real good meals at the Palace Cafe in the past couple of months, and whatever that mail shovin'ism is, she smiled when she said it.

Miss Sue Etta Bruff must of thought she was going to church or something, because when she showed up for the flight she had on her best outfit, including a flimsy blouse that looked like it was made out of Kleenex. She had a buncha trouble getting up into General Doolittle—that's what Uncle Milo calls his plane—but finally she squeezed in and smiled at Uncle Milo like they were real good friends. Then he gunned the engine.

That ol' plane shot into the air like a cork out of a bottle, and everybody in town rushed out into the street to wave.

About the time they leveled off at the head of Main Street they found out they had a third passenger in the plane. There's this family of wild honey bees in that old tin shed at the airport where Uncle Milo keeps General Doolittle. Apparently, one of them bees thought it'd be a picnic to take a ride in Miss Sue Etta Bruff's flouncy blouse.

We heard her squall clean over the roar of that old engine. Of course, nobody on the ground knew what was actually happening, and most were afraid to ask. All we could see was her laying all over Uncle Milo and yanking at her clothes. She'd rammed Uncle Milo's seat forward and was clawing at her blouse and yelling fit to die. Just as she squealed and smashed Uncle Milo's head up against the front of the cockpit for the third time, she stood straight up in the wind and her blouse flew off like it was paper.

Miss Sue Etta Bruff kept on screaming as Uncle Milo banked his plane and flew it straight onto the Cedar Gap Veterans' Memorial Airport runway. Everybody must have been watching, because they jumped in whatever would run and bounced out to the airport. We found Uncle Milo walking away from General Doolittle sorta unsteady, one hand on a black eye, the other holding back a little stream of blood we found out later came from Miss Sue Etta Bruff when she hit him with one of them spike heels of hers.

"Where's Sue Etta?" somebody yelled.

Uncle Milo nodded toward the plane. "She's hunkered down in the cockpit, waitin' for somebody to bring her some more clothes." He wobbled off toward his pickup truck.

You know, Mrs. Orabone, I coulda made some good money from this streamy-conscience writing. Uncle Milo offered me fifty cents just to list all the things Miss Sue Etta Bruff called him when she was grabbing for that bee.

I asked him, "Ain't you and her sorta going together?"

"Actually, Turnbow," Uncle Milo said, "me 'n Sue Etta, we ain't near as close as we used to be. Write your paper."

But my mama said that in streamy-conscience writing you oughta emphasize the conscience over the streamy, so I can't use all those truly fine words.

Boy, there were some good-uns!

CHAPTER 3

ANIMALS MIGHT NEAR HUMAN

AT THE GAP

Talkin' to the Animals

As a general rule, Cedar Gapians don't vote important verdicts without careful analysis. It's not their inherited style. They take their time, cogitate the history of the problem, contemplate the players, meditate on the benefits of a decision, reflect on the potential pain, and only then do they come down with a definitive appraisal.

Just the other day we finally got a focus on something that's been a tremendous bother to many people for some time, namely, the humanoid characteristics of our livestock.

"I truly hate to bring this up," Gunther Burns said, "but we've got a few people in this town who think their pets talk back to them."

The Palace Cafe crowd erupted in pro and con arguments. Luther "20–20" Gravely, hearing words that impinged on his field of psychoanalysis, carefully opened his bloodshot eyes. "We trained professionals call that *anthropomorphism*." He looked around, proud of negotiating the minefield of a six-syllable word. "We also call it hogwash."

"It ain't to some people, Luther," Lester Goodrich said. "You've seen that fat poodle of Eunice and Francine's. They talk to that useless mutt like it can understand English and French both." For at least fifteen years, the elderly Riddleberry sisters have discussed everything from politics to the Rapture with their lardy poodle, Jean-Claude. "Did you know Francine swears that mutt only barks in Old Gallic."

All of the men nodded and pointed at each other as if that proved their point. Bertie Faye Hogg, our postmistress, glowered at Lester. "Now, look," she said, "pets have unique communicative skills." When the men laughed and shook their heads, Bertie Faye's squeaky voice dropped an octave. "I'm telling you, my cat Boopsie not only understands what I'm saying, she reads my mind."

"Whyn't you teach her to read Zip codes," Corley Freemont muttered, "so's our mail could get to Houston in under a month?"

Jakub Mielczewski, our Polish connection, stirred his coffee solemnly. "I have onkle in Krakow with counting mouse." There was a long silence, then quick glances from the listeners. "Onkle cannot count, so mouse must do it for him." Jake took another deep drink of his coffee.

Brenda Beth Kollwood, our finest Palace Cafe waitress, said quietly, "I think Luther sweetened Mr. Mielczewski's coffee a bit more than normal."

Luther and Jake often celebrate unusual events—like sighting a dented pickup or discovering that the sun has come up—by swilling coffee cut with Luther's personal designer hooch. Jake's augmented coffee often takes him on a straight line from coy invincibility to intercontinental telepathy.

Silas Eddardson, the lone professor at the Cedar Gap Conservatory of Music, smiled at the ceiling, his eyes closed in beatific worship. "Did you know," he said with precision, "that Franz Schubert composed a song honoring a trout? Very touching. You can almost hear the trout's thoughts."

"There you go," Bertie Faye said. "If Silas's trout can think, then my cat can talk."

Silas's thinking trout would have ended the discussion, except Arnold Curnutt idly mentioned that his wife once talked to some baby rabbits she found in her yard. "I truly think Dodie expected them to talk back to her."

Dodie carefully set down her coffee cup. "Is that anything like you talking to Cannonball?"

"Aw, Honey, you know that's different." Cannonball, Arnold's old hound, boasts the sorriest quail-sighting record of any dog in town, including Jean-Claude.

"Cannonball, unless my memory fails, is a dog, and you were talking to him. How's that different?"

"Because he understands. Anyway, I just talk to him about bird hunting. It wouldn't be no use atall to talk to him about anything else, like bein' a sheep dog."

"You *talk* to him about hunting?"

The men looked puzzled. "Yeah," Lester Goodrich said, "ever'-body does that, don't they?" He glanced at the nodding heads. "What's so unusual?"

Dodie, Bertie Faye, and three previously silent women laughed derisively. Dodie shook her head. "Cannonball is a *dog!*"

"Aw, naw, Honey, he's not just your average mutt. Cannonball's a *bird* dog. There's a big, *big* difference. You see, Cannonball has all those generations of fine huntin' blood in him. He's not like that useless poodle of Eunice and Francine's. Cannonball *knows!* When I tell him we're only lookin' for dove, and to leave the quail alone, he understands."

Dodie shook her head slowly. "And he answers?"

"Naaaaaw! He doesn't say anything." Arnold looked around and shrugged, as if his wife had slipped a gear. "He just nods."

Every male head bobbed vigorously. "Right!" Corley Freemont shouted. "We've all seen our dogs do that. I tell my ol' blue tick hound things I'd never tell a wife. If I had a wife."

"Which," Dodie said as she exited, "is an early warning to any potential wives in the neighborhood."

A peculiar silence descended on the Palace Cafe. The men looked around bewildered.

"You know," Arnold said, obviously mystified, "I don't think those women believed us!"

Buttercup's Last Ride

Anybody who's spent any time at all around livestock realizes that you learn to read animal glances or else you learn to run real fast. Although some foreigners—say, people from Capetown or Minneapolis—believe otherwise, there are occasions when farm animals do find things amusing, get ticked off, listen to crickets, or become confused. Just like humans.

Right now, two of our young boys are extremely busy performing a very long series of unrewarding odd jobs while they contemplate their recent zoological education. The work is for money and for penance; the education was serendipitous. Although all are related to the calf incident, the money goes to Luther Gravely for his professional time as a psychologist.

The calf thing started when Travis Breedlow decided the time had come to separate his old milk cow, Bonnie Blue, from her calf, Buttercup. Besides taking all of Bonnie Blue's milk, Buttercup was worrying the poor old cow into a nervous tic. Travis announced to his family, "We just need to keep that calf off to herself and busy for a week or two so she can learn the beauty of a grass diet."

At that instant Travis's fifth-grade boy, Howie, got this glint to his eyes. All the next day Howie doodled in his math book as he thought about his daddy's statement. Finally, right at the dismissal bell, he grinned. That afternoon he dragged his seven-year-old brother, Joe Billy, down to their barn where Howie lifted some old leather reins off a stable wall.

"Come on, Joe Billy, we got some work to do."

"I don't want to do no work."

"Come on, you'll like this. We're gonna keep that calf busy."

Joe Billy, a chubby second grader, would rather, if he has his choice, watch the clouds change shapes. "I dunno, Howie. Maybe Daddy won't like it."

"Naw, we're doin' for Daddy. You heard him plain as day say we needed to keep the calf busy for a couple of weeks." Howie glared at his wavering brother.

Joe Billy hesitated. "How we gonna do it?"

Howie squinted toward Buttercup, who was dogging Bonnie Blue's every step. "We're gonna harness her to that Radio Flyer wagon of ours."

Joe Billy's mouth dropped open. "We cain't do that! We'll all be killed for sure!"

"Naw! Buttercup's even lazier than you are. All we're gonna do is tie a piece of this leather around her neck, then run it down both sides to our wagon, just like on a horse." He thunked his brother on the head. "Go get the wagon."

It took the better part of an hour to tie up the skittish calf, but finally Howie finished the improvised harness. "OK, Joe Billy, get in."

"I ain't gonna ride alone!" Joe Billy yelled, backpedaling.

Howie rolled his eyes. "Hey, dry up! We're both goin'! I'll just straddle you."

They got settled; then Howie pulled the long rope attached to the slipknot holding Buttercup. When the rope fell away, the calf stood waggling her head at the unfamiliar leather encircling her. It might have worked if Howie hadn't seen so many old Hopalong Cassidy movies on cable. He slapped the improvised reins and yelled, "Get up!"

Buttercup mistook the harness for some kind of killer bobcat clawing at her. She bleated like a mountain diesel and then took off at a high-tailed dead run straight into a stand of spiny shinnery and young mesquite bushes. The thorny branches whipped at the two terrified boys, who screamed like banshees, enraging Bonnie Blue, who had been shuffling around nearby, watching the proceedings.

With the delicate touch of a crazed bull elephant, Bonnie Blue took out at an angle through the brambles, searching for her baby. Her bawling bass and Buttercup's strangled tenor finally joined in a thicket of dead Johnson grass and wild grape vines covering an old rusty fence. That much beef traveling with that velocity guaranteed that something was going to give.

With a tremendous grunt Bonnie Blue crashed through the fence line, knocking Buttercup in a complete circle and causing rusty wire to sing through staples for two hundred yards in both directions. The Radio Flyer wagon with its screeching occupants slid under the calf. Buttercup, knowing for sure that the bobcat had grown into a snarling two-headed mountain lion, promptly relieved herself on the wagon and then sat on it.

Dry weeds, rotten fence posts, red clay, and fresh manure mixed in about equal portions as the terrified boys clawed their way from under the calf's flailing hooves. Bonnie Blue attempted to comfort her baby by alternately bawling and licking.

When the dust settled and everybody recognized everybody else, the battered and scratched boys retrieved their flattened wagon, Bonnie Blue ambled toward home with an even more confused look than usual, and Buttercup had supper.

Travis Breedlow sat nursing a cup of Palace Cafe coffee and shaking his head. "Luther said he was available if the money was right."

"What's Luther got to do with it?" somebody asked.

"Well, the whole thing made Bonnie Blue go dry as a stump. Those boys are tryin' to hire Luther to psychoanalyze the pore ol' cow and get her back on track givin' her gallon a day."

"Luther works with animals?"

"Well, Luther said he was as good with cows as he was with people." Travis looked around. "Whatta ya think?"

There was a lot of throat clearing. Nobody wanted to touch that one.

A Bad Case of Cat

Several months ago a dead mouse in Gunther Burns's two-story vintage house almost required the house's demolition. Two weeks later Gunther, without thinking, chased another family of mice into a hole under his porch. He stalked in the Palace Cafe, promising death and destruction to anything with fur—a prophetic curse.

"Hey, Gunther," Carter Burkhalter said, "whyn't you go over to Ambrosio's and get one a them cats from out behind his repair shop?" Ambrosio Gonzales, our intuitive mechanical genius from Chihuahua, Mexico, keeps several cats to hold down the rodent population in his "inventory."

Gunther chewed on his mustache. "Hmm. Reckon I could catch one?"

Carter shrugged. "Trap it, maybe. Grab one with your hands, and you'll lose about an acre of skin."

"They that mean?"

"Those cats left mean at birth. They're up to fiendish and moving toward bloodthirsty. Get Ambrosio to help. He knows his livestock."

An hour later Gunther plopped a wire cage next to his back porch. Inside the cage hunkered the scrawniest, snarlingest full-grown gray and black cat he'd ever seen.

"That cat's not much for looks," Esther said, frowning.

Gunther peered over his glasses. "You wanta see the Band-Aids where I tried to pick him up?" He placed the cage against an opening in the porch foundation, and then slid the cage door open. "Ambrosio finally trapped him. Said he was the best mouser of the litter."

"Looks too small." Esther shook her head. "Runts are generally weak."

Gunther sighed as he related the story. "The cat was pretty suspicious. Then I guess he got a good strong whiff of mouse because he squalled and shot under that porch like a surface-to-air missile."

Ten minutes later the cat proudly laid three mice at the cage door.

"That cat musta got a religious call," Gunther sighed, "because it took off through the innards of my house, crawling straight up through the walls and under every floor like a preacher after a backslider."

Esther rolled her eyes. "It was that way for two days. At night we'd hear him scratching across our ceiling. At every meal that cat would race up inside the wall right by our table, screeching like a mountain lion. There'd be a little squeak, and five minutes later the cat would push another dead mouse into the cage."

For forty-eight hours straight the cat stalked, squalled and pounced. Esther and Gunther tried coaxing the cat out with milk and cat food, and finally pure cream. They even fried up some catfish fingers as bait. "But that cat shot into and outa the cage before I could slam the cage door."

Then Wednesday night the worst possible thing happened: the cat ran out of mice. For two days this pitiful screen-door squeaking sound could be heard as the cat trailed across the Burns's bedroom ceiling, crawled slowly straight up inside the wall next to their TV, or slithered under their breakfast table.

"We figured, well, it'll come out when it gets hungry." Gunther shook his head in frustration. "Wrong!"

"The cat still there?" somebody asked.

Gunther shook his head. "When I told Ambrosio, he just grinned and pulled something out of that ol' refrigerator he keeps in the back of his shop. He walked over to my back porch and shoved a small flat can onto the floor of the cage. Then he stood with a broom handle on the cage door."

The meowing turned into a screeching clatter that trailed down the wall and across the second floor. Suddenly, the cat plopped onto the dirt under the house and zipped into the cage and began eating from the small can, unmindful of Ambrosio's clicking the cage door shut.

"Ambrosio's cat's back at the Old Chihuahua Repair Shop," Gunther sighed, "and me 'n Esther's lookin' forward to some catless sleep."

We waited. Finally, Milo Shively leaned forward. "Well?"

Gunther looked up. "Well, what?"

Milo threw up his hands. "What was in the can?"

"Oh. That." Gunther shrugged. "Refried beans. Ambrosio's brother-in-law accidently brought the cat up in a load of cantaloupe from Matamoros. The only thing it'll eat is mice and refried beans."

As Milo said, "Seems a tad high in protein. You reckon the Food and Drug Administration's got a minimum daily requirement chart for either mice or refried beans?"

Government being what it is, we're afraid to mention it. The next thing we know, we'll have three federal biologists doing a study in Ambrosio's junkyard.

The Law of the Jungle

While home teaching isn't commonly recognized as a blood sport, it has its downside. Carter Burkhalter found that out when he undertook the organic education of his granddaughter.

Treesie May, Carter's first grandchild, is a bright-eyed first grader with the fey spirit of a butterfly. That's where her adult education began.

Yancy McWhirter saw Carter shaking his head over a cup of Palace Cafe coffee. "Hey, Carter, I see your granddaughter's stayin' with you this weekend. She's a cute one. How's she doin'?"

Carter shrugged. "Aw, Treesie May's healthy and bright enough, but she's too nicey-nice." He looked around. "Ya know what I mean? She won't play in the mud, or crawl around in a dusty hayloft, or walk through a horse lot. It's like she's afraid of bein' an average kid."

"You can forget anything with dirt or a smell," Carter muttered. "But the worst problem is with killin' animals we're goin' to eat. She runs inside ever' time I head for the chicken coop."

Like most normal adults, Carter has long since realized that death is an integral part of life, and in the larger scheme of things some animals will die. When Treesie May came to Carter's house for the weekend, Carter made a clenched-jaw resolution that before the weekend was out his granddaughter would learn that dirt and death are part of living.

"Yesterday I kept up a chatter about goin' fishin' for bass and crappie out in Sybil's stock tank. We were goin' to use worms for bait. I figured workin' with a worm and a fish would be a good way to start."

Everybody grinned and nodded. "For your basic nasty, a worm'll sure break the ice," Milo Shively said. "Particularly night crawlers."

Carter spread his hands in frustration. "Sure, they'd have been the best if I could get her to pick 'em up! I had to do all the baiting. And then when she finally caught a fish, she wouldn't even touch it. She said it was . . . 'yuckie!' "

"Now, don't be too hard on her, Carter," Brenda Beth Kollwood said. "Little girls are different than hard-ankle boys. It just takes a little while longer."

"It only took fifteen minutes," Carter said, looking around.

Everybody leaned close. "You mean you got Treesie May to bait a hook?"

"Better'n that," Carter said.

Grandfather and granddaughter, the experienced and the innocent, sat quietly on the bank eating their sandwiches and watching the corks bob. Suddenly, a movement in some dry weeds caught Treesie May's eye. "Look, Grandpa, a butterfly!"

"It's wings are movin' awful slow," Carter said. "Maybe you better not try to . . ."

But Treesie May was already on her knees. "It looks like he's caught on a twig, Grandpa. Maybe I can . . ."

Her sudden squeal shocked Carter. The girl jumped toward her grandfather and grabbed him while she sucked in and gasped out her breath too fast to make a sound.

"What's the matter, Baby?" Carter said. "Did you touch a thorn?"

"Look . . . at the . . . butterfly," she sobbed. "It doesn't . . . have a head!"

Carter gazed at the butterfly through his bifocals. The headless butterfly's wings moved lazily, guided by some non-cranial memory. Then Carter looked closer. Where the butterfly had been he saw what at first looked like a dead twig. Then he saw a tan walking stick, a relative of the praying mantis, back slowly under a leaf, its meal interrupted.

It took Carter almost an hour to talk the sobs away from his granddaughter. Eventually her curiosity and her grandfather's warm arms forced her to see the beautiful butterfly as only part of a chain. "The butterfly eats little bugs," Carter told her gently, "the walking stick eats butterflies, chickens eat walking sticks, we eat chickens."

The Palace Cafe crowd quieted at this reenactment of the oldest rule in the books. "It's a hard lesson," Carter said, "but now Treesie May knows that if you want bacon with your eggs, somebody's ol' pig is gonna draw the black bean."

"Is she OK now?" Brenda Beth asked as she splashed coffee in ignored cups.

"Yeah, she's fine." Carter drew in a deep breath. "My only problem now is to answer her last question."

We waited.

"Oh, you know," he said finally. "If we eat the chicken, what's gonna eat us?"

SATURDAY'S JOURNAL

ZOUNDS, THE HOUNDS

OF PERDITION!

nd, truly, the seventh day being come, the burghers of the fair village of Gap-in-the-Cedar did gather near the hostelry and alehouse unjustly named after a palace. To be righteously true, we must report that there was much nervous glancing over shoulders and behind carts, even an occasional, "Hark, hearest thou a hound?"

What began as a gentle week quickly took on the image of Master Milton's Purgatorium due to an innocent effort by one of our honest workers, Yeoman Bubba by name.

Tuesday last, it was, that one of Bubba's two hounds gave the appearance of having been attacked by an evil nose-running demon. This hound, which answereth to the name of Hawk—the other hound's name is, perforce, Spit—could but lay around loglike and snore raucously.

"Hound," Bubba said, "ere this day is far spent, thou shalt have a physic for thy lethargy." Hawk, his spirit unmoved, drooled on the dusty floor.

Rather than rouse Squire Greenslope, the local dispenser of bitter herbs, Yeoman Bubba pawed through a rude shelf filled with dusty pouches and boxes containing half-a-life's worth of nostrums.

Suddenly Bubba gave a little cry. "Aha! A pouch of powder from my youth." He furrowed his brow as he sorted through strands of memory, attempting to dredge up the powder's exact abilities. "It was either for a runny nose," he said, frowning, "or to loosen the bark on our elm tree." Bubba's strands of memory run toward the frazzled.

He quickly mixed the powder with water, and then carefully lifted Hawk's limp upper lip. "Old Hawk, with this thou art on the mend." As he poured half the nostrum into Hawk's comatose mouth, Spit ambled loosely into Bubba's cluttered hut. "Heigh, ho, Old Spit. Hast thou a demon also? We shall kill it ere it rears its fangéd head." So saying, he dribbled the remaining liquid in the mouth of the yawning Spit.

Although it was not known at that time, the powder, having aged in the pouch for a decade or more, had taken on several mutant characteristics. Originally an energy restorative for their huge dray horse, a pinch was the suggested measure for the powder, not a full pouch.

Strange lightninglike charges flickered through the soggy brains of the two hounds. Suddenly Hawk's eyes flew open. Against the far sod wall he imagined he spied something very large with wings and feathers. His confused mind refused to process the information that objects the size of Bubba's bed seldom came with wings and feathers. With a keening snarl, Hawk grabbed the six-foot-long straw-filled imaginary bird . . . just as the largest snake in his memory flowed through their ancient oak tree and squirmed toward the river.

Despite the royal dog blood flowing in his veins, the hound realized that attacking that snakish varmint was pure suicide. Since ritual self-immolation was not his style, Hawk attempted to escape by launching himself through Bubba's tiny window. The closed tiny window high on the dirt wall.

As Yeoman Bubba later described it, "Although Noble Hawk smashed one paw and his head through my window, his remaining paws clawed my dirt wall like an armadillo after a bug." Sure that the imaginary giant snake was upon him, the hound wailed and its traditionally bass voice turned into a terrified mouselike squeaking.

This confused Spit, who could see nothing unusual in the scene other than the fact that both he and Hawk were underwater.

To save his buddy from drowning, Spit clamped down on Hawk's tail. Then he swam valiantly toward the surface of his mystical lake. Hawk, knowing for sure that the giant snake had him in its fiery jaws, yowled and clawed all the harder.

When a huge hole appeared in Bubba's sod hovel, the two dogs rolled through it into the street and from thence into the Palace Alehouse where their frothing minds transformed the rum-soaked and snoring Squire Gravely into an alligator (Spit's version) or an unbelievably attractive lady hound (Hawk's version). The two snarled, rolled, yelped and tore up the alehouse's entire kitchen as Spit attempted to escape the snapping teeth of his green monster while Hawk strove valiantly to return the lady hound's advances.

Eventually the powder ran its course, of course. But all can never be as before. To this hour Hawk lurches around bleary-eyed, searching for the gorgeous, panting lady hound. Spit, consumed with alligator nightmares, sleeps uneasily on top of Bubba's trashed hut. Bubba considers the view from his gaping window as "breezy, but otherwise much improved."

But hark, Squire Gravely's rum-sotted voice soundeth yet another version of his being set upon by "forty slavering demons with bad breath and unseemly amorous intentions." Like all truly classic tales, his chronicle improves with comradeship, liquid fueling, and repetition.

But enough of our historical peregrinations. We must away!

CHAPTER 4

EVILS OF THE WEED

Does the Surgeon General Know about This?

One day recently, Wade and Hershel Lutton, Tom Lutton's oldest boys, and Son Jacobs's boy, Patrick, found themselves with that dangerous adolescent commodity, an unspoken-for afternoon. What followed was in the classic mold of other disasters like the Johnstown flood and the Edsel.

Hershel led the way off the four o'clock school bus. "Hey, Wade," Hershel yelled. "Let's go get a D.P."

Wade looked around and grinned. "I got a better idea." Hershel and Pat turned, curious. "Tell ya in the clubhouse." They ran to a deserted barn and scrambled up a crude ladder into the loft. Slowly, Wade pulled an unopened pack of cigarettes from his jacket pocket.

"Wow!" Hershel whispered. "Where'd ya get those?"

"Found 'em in the bathroom at school."

"Whatta ya gonna do with 'em?" Pat asked.

Wade looked at the younger boy as if he were a brain-damaged goat. "Smoke them, of course." He frowned. "You can, too, if you're man enough."

Hershel and Pat glanced quickly at each other, and then at Wade. Pat shook his head. "My daddy'll kill me if he finds out I been messin' with cigarettes."

"It's OK if you chicken out," Wade said, shrugging. "Me 'n Hershel can finish the pack by ourselves."

Hershel's mouth dropped open. But a brother's challenge simply could not be ignored. "Yeah," Hershel said, "me 'n Wade can handle those ciggies by ourselves."

Pat licked his lips. He squinted at the forbidden fruit. "Hold it right there! You're not gonna smoke my cigs. If this is a club, then those are part mine. Right?"

"Right," Wade said, zipping the cellophane off the pack. "Since I got the only match, I get the first light."

Three pairs of eyes flashed as the match flared. Wade sucked in, and then coughed violently. Tears streamed from his eyes. But he quickly straightened and sighed. "Nice!" He looked around. "Who's next?"

Hershel held out a tentative hand. "Uh, I'll try one of those." He put his cigarette against the glowing end of Wade's. Finally he blew out a tiny blue cloud. "Hey, this is all right!"

Soon all three were blowing smoke rings and practicing holding the cigarettes between various combinations of fingers. Wade tried it like a Commie spy he'd seen once in a movie. Then Pat minced around holding the cigarette like a society matron.

Unfortunately, the boys' tolerance for nicotine was about equivalent to Rambo's tolerance for Iranians. The little springs under their tongues began bubbling up just as their mouths reached the approximate taste of smouldering burlap.

Pat crumbled first. "I think I better . . ." The sentence died as he lost his lunch and breakfast all over his books. Hershel might have made it, except Pat's bent-over retching triggered a sympathetic response.

Wade, figuring things had taken a serious downturn, edged toward the ladder. Halfway down, his own unbiased attraction for nicotine topped out. He hung by one hand as he joined the Brotherhood of the Instantly Smarter.

When they finally staggered home, it took Tom Lutton about three seconds to analyze the scene. "I'll handle it, Eileen." He turned to Wade. "Looks like a touch of the flu, Son. Tell ya what I always found helpful. A big, raw onion. Best thing for the flu."

Wade's analytical ability had pegged on zero. He thought he'd fooled his father. He pawed weakly through the refrigerator until he found an old, gnarled onion. He was into his third bite before the onion juice and the nicotine mixed. He immediately lost the rest of whatever might be hanging around in his stomach.

Tom smiled as he told the story. "My daddy used that onion trick on me. It cured me for years."

Lester Goodrich set down his coffee. "I hate to berate the afflicted, but it kinda serves them right for messin' with real tobacco."

"Yeah," Waldo Beeler said. "They should have stuck with cedar bark like the rest of us used."

"Aw, cedar bark's for beginners," Lester said. "Actually, mesquite root's the best, but you gotta dry it just right."

Monroe Sternly shook his head. "You sissies never tried grapevine."

"Well, grapevine draws good," Murphy Gumpton said, "but it'll burn your tongue so's you won't taste anything for a week. Best thing's coffee grounds."

The conversation degenerated pretty fast from there. Somebody should have given those ol' boys more onions.

Ya Just Gotta Plan Ahead to Quit the Weed

More onions would definitely have helped. At least it would have cut into the series of 140-hour days experienced by the three survivors of the Great Cedar Gap Smokeout.

The whole thing started with a notice on the bulletin board at the Palace Hotel and Cafe:

> *It's nasty! It's expensive! It'll kill ya!*
> *Free coffee for a year for anybody*
> *brave enough to stop smoking.*

"I remember when I quit back in '62," Yancy McWhirter said. "No trouble a tall. Piece a cake."

Nobody reminded Yancy of that ghastly summer of 1962 when for two months his gimlet-eyed stare cleared a path down our sidewalk like a jaguar stalking through a rabbit farm.

Although several people bragged of their ability either to take tobacco or leave it be, by sundown the team of quitters had been narrowed to three, Newt Jimson, Corley Freemont and Stafford Higginbotham. Each declared he would have the toughest time because of the frazzling strain generated by his profession.

"Listen, I work twelve-hour days out at the Gas-N-Git, an' you cain't imagine the pressure of never knowin' who'll come through that door or what'll be wrong with the car." He looked longingly at the pack of Luckies he'd just thrown on the table. "We're talkin' major stress."

"Stress?" Corley sneered. Corley coaches everything down at our South Taylor County Junior College. "I'll show you stress. Get your football team ready for a playoff game. Then on Friday you find out that both linebackers flunked, the only defensive lineman over 136 pounds broke his leg, and the quarterback ran off with the dean's daughter. I tell ya, that'd make Mother Teresa take up cigars."

"Well, you babies," Hig muttered. "Just hang out with me an' my propane truck. Then remember that a little backfire or spark of static electricity can turn the whole truck an' you with it into a three-ton cherry bomb firecracker. Think about *that* later an' you'll get the shakes for sure."

True enough, Hig's finger tremors are legendary. When he plays pool the cue tip blurs like a hummingbird's wings, and his signature resembles a San Andreas Fault seismograph readout. No one remembers him without a cigarette dangling from his lips, a thread of smoke curling up into his half-closed eyes.

But all three took the pledge last Saturday.

Sunday was troublesome, but prayer and gluttony pulled them through. Pastor Eldred Simpson at the Baptist Church shook his head. "Brother Jimson's eyes glimmered like a cornered rattler, but he only ripped out three pages flipping through his hymnal."

Monday, Corley tore up a tackling dummy he'd used through ten seasons. "Just workin' off a little tension," he said sheepishly. "I guess they don't make quarter-inch steel like they used to."

Meanwhile, Hig was as serene as a Zen breakfast. His smile gleamed, his coffee hand was rock-steady, and his speech patterns echoed with both humanity and humility. "Boy, ol' Newt and Corley are sure going through some bad times. I truly feel for 'em."

Few things are more irritating than public pity. Thursday, Corley ran his fist through a water fountain that gurgled too loudly. Friday, Newt screamed at Eunice and Francine Riddleberry, two elderly unmarried sisters, accusing them of several unnatural proclivities, two of which were physically impossible.

Yesterday was to be the magic morning, the theory running that on the seventh day nicotine loses its hold on the user. Newt and Corley were haggard from loss of sleep and the knowledge they had verbally assaulted half the citizens of Cedar Gap as well as physically abused several hundred dollars worth of inanimate objects.

Hig, on the other hand, smiled gently at the waitress, waved at the assembled crowd, and called for a nice cup of tea. "Tea is so civilized, don'tcha think?" Corley's gritted teeth sounded like rocks on a tin roof. Newt gripped a plastic bottle of syrup until it exploded onto the ceiling.

The upshot is that all three are apparently off the weed. Today they even managed to shake hands at their group success. Or they did until Hig grinned. "Actually, I gave up cigarettes about two months ago."

"Naw, ya didn't," Newt said. "I seen ya smokin'."

"For thirty years, yep, but for two months, nope! I decided it was time, so I just quit without tellin' anybody."

Corley and Newt looked at each other, muttered something about truck drivers with reptilian characteristics, and stalked out. On the way Corley brushed against the Rotarian's gum machine. We held our breaths. Corley glared, but walked on.

The gum machine survived. The spotlight on the volunteer firetruck outside didn't.

SATURDAY'S JOURNAL

THE VIEW FROM THE TREE

ell, it's Saturday here in Cedar Gap and the vigil is over. The little 2 × 4 seat in the Aubrey's pecan tree is down. And the flag's gone.

A couple of Sundays ago, Bryce and Bobbie Lynn Aubrey were on a drive out to their little half-section ranch when Richie, their chubby-faced fifth grader, spied a baby coon. As he leapt out of the pickup, he tripped and fell headfirst into a boulder-filled creek.

When Bryce and Bobbie Lynn carried Richie home from the hospital, their son was in an open-eyed coma. They moved him into their front upstairs bedroom looking out over the front yard and the big Burkett pecan tree. The wind-up bed allowed his uncomprehending eyes to peer out at the tree he'd climbed hundreds of times.

Within the hour a timid knock sounded on the Aubrey's front door. Bryce opened the door to find a skinny, freckle-faced boy, serious and agitated, looking up at him. "Yes, Toober?"

"Mr. Aubrey, me 'n these guys"—he nodded over his shoulder at three of Richie's chums—"thought, maybe, if 'n it's OK with you 'n Richie, we might climb up in your ol' pecan tree an' sorta keep

Richie company." When Bryce started to object, Toober Wormsley's eyes got very large. "Oh, we won't say nothin'. We'll just sit there." He shrugged. "We won't even wave, if you don't think it right."

Bryce's eyes started to fill. "Well, Toober, I appreciate the offer, and I'm sure Richie would, too, but he's, well, he's not able to wake up right now. He can't . . ." Then he felt the friendship of the quartet sweep across the doorway like heat from a fireplace. He nodded. "Sure. Go ahead. I guess it's OK."

Toober, Tom Lee Studer, Hermando Salazar, and Delores Ann Herberson backed quietly off the porch. Bryce watched as they conferred, heads bent together. Finally they all got out coins, flipped, and then Tom Lee slowly climbed the old tree.

At about eye-level with Richie's room, Tom Lee tied a short 2 × 4 across a forked branch with some clothesline rope. He tested it, then settled himself, folded his hands, and began staring at Richie's window. For three hours he never moved. Then Hermando climbed up and repeated the quiet watch until relieved by Delores Ann. There was no waving or calling out, just a silent honor guard by friends who could not understand what had happened but figured their buddy might be lonesome.

They left when the sun went down, but by sunup they were back. This time each brought something they thought Richie might like— a yo-yo, a softball bat, a frizbee they'd played with at recess, and finally a flag made from a torn sheet with "Capt. Richie Get Well" painted with neon orange.

None of the four asked to come inside. They'd heard chilling stories about Richie's blank stare and the tubes taped to his arms. That was too much to ask, even from friends. But sitting in the old pecan tree, in the fork where they'd tied swings and hung upside-down, that they could do. And they could see Richie, albeit dimly, through the mullioned window as he lay propped up, gray flesh against white sheets.

The second day the comic books appeared, *Archie* and *Sgt. Rock* and *Superboy*. Delores Ann carried a science fiction book she knew Richie liked, reading it silently but turning it around every few minutes so Richie could see the fantastic illustrations. And all the time the Capt. Richie flag fluttered from its clothesline flagpole.

Two days ago, while Toober sat guard on the tree seat, a car suddenly pulled to the curb. Doc Winslow shuffled quickly inside. As if answering some unheard call, Tom Lee, Hermando, and Delores Ann wandered in from various parts of town. Like children throughout history, they watched as the grown-ups did whatever it was grown-ups had to do in times of stress.

The four stood quietly as Bryce walked to Richie's window, looked down at them, and then slowly lowered the old shade, darkening the window.

Toober blinked back some tears as he stared down at his three remaining friends. They looked back, helpless and confused. Finally Hermando pointed to the flag. Toober nooded. He lowered the flag halfway, and then tied it firmly to the forked branch.

The flag stayed at half-mast through the funeral service. We don't know where it is right now, but we think it's buried somewhere up on the mesa, probably in a secret cedar brake, underneath a flat stone with something like "Good-bye, Capt. Richie" scratched on it.

CHAPTER 5

INDIVIDUAL INITIATIVE

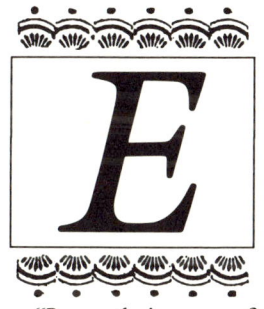

Beat of a Different Drummer

Every day last June, Calvin Kinchlow rattled his eighty-four-year-old bones out to the red oak in his front yard. He'd been watching a nest of five new swallowtails gradually grow until they overflowed their tea cup-sized swirl of twigs and weeds.

"I saw their mama feedin' them, so I grabbed for my binoculars. Four of those little jaspers were facin' right up to their mama's worm-filled beak, their mouths open like mousetraps. That other baby bird was facin' directly away, 180 degrees from the easy food. He was eyein' a better bug on a leaf just out of his reach." Calvin squinched up his face, the nearest to a smile he ever gets. "That's my kinda bird."

Every crowd has someone like that. There's a yell, somebody points at the sky, and every head but one looks up, gape-mouthed and excited. That one dissenting head will be frowning at the pointer and thinking, "I'm pretty sure I could have yelled that a little bit better."

There are occasional problems with those sorts of people, like driving parents to drink or teachers out of the profession. On the other hand, they're more fun to watch, and sometimes they're even right.

That special kind of individual Cedar Gap initiative is the reason Corley Freemont, the coach of everything down at South Taylor County Junior College, bought coffee for Jasper Hungerford, our one-man STCJC music department.

To look at Jap Hungerford, the conductor of the STCJC Fighting Gila Monster Band, you'd never realize that under that prematurely bald thirty-five-year-old musician's skull festers the mind of a lonely samurai warrior. Early this week Jap heard Corley grousing to some other faculty members in the faculty lounge.

"I cain't believe that Billy Gannison," Corley muttered. "He's got about as much sense of timing as thunder."

Jap slouched quietly onto a folding chair.

"What's Gannison's problem?" somebody asked.

"His problem," Corley said through clenched teeth, "is any race over one lap long. He could run from here to El Paso if he paced himself, but he blows everything on the first lap." Corley shrugged helplessly. "Then he just slouches along like a dog in a rainstorm."

Jap squinted in concentration. Gannison, he thought. Where have I heard that name?

"Billy Gannison," a vice-president asked. "Isn't he that kid with legs about nine feet long? Walks like he's on stilts?"

"You nailed him." Corley clenched his fists in frustration. "Runs the same way. His problem is, he tries to match steps with those little bitty milers from Hereford Junior College and San Angelo Bible Academy, but his stride is normally about a foot longer so he wears out. If he doesn't do that, then he gets the same fast rhythm as those other runners, and then he winds up a hunnert yards ahead after one lap. Then he dies."

"Can't you tell him to stay back in the pack?"

Corley shook his head sadly. "Won't work. He says he loses the beat."

Jasper analyzed Corley's last sentence. "Corley," he said slowly, "excuse me for interruptin', but do you mind if I watch your boy work out this week?"

"Help yourself. Just don't cry when you see the tragedy."

For the next three afternoons, Jap sat by himself in the bleachers while he scrutinized Billy Gannison's gangling water-bird form limbering up, stomping through some exercises, and then racing around the track. Jap chewed on a piece of grass as he ambled back toward the World War II barracks housing the STCJC music building. Then he snapped his fingers. He turned toward Old Main and the students' permanent records. Thirty minutes later he walked out, smiling slyly.

Friday afternoon Jap assembled his eighteen available band members on the bleachers.

"Hey, Prof, why we doin' a track gig?"

"Never mind," Jap said. "Just keep that music in the right order and when I give the downbeat, play loud."

Finally the announcer yelled, "For the mile run, Wilson for the Hereford Bulls, Plummer for San Angelo Bible, and Gannison for the Fighting Gila Monsters!" Jap stood up and snapped his fingers. "Get ready with 'Bridge Over Troubled Waters.' We're takin' it fast!"

At the pistol shot, Jap waited until the runners settled into a steady stride, then he snapped his fingers four times and nodded. His motley remnant blazed away on horns and drums, exactly matching the strides of the runners. Then, carefully but steadily, Jap slowed down the tempo until what had been a quick step became a plodding exercise in musical monotony.

Jap glanced at Billy Gannison's spindly legs pumping slowly far back in the pack. "Perfect," he muttered.

Just as the runners passed the stands at the end of the first lap, Jap yelled, "'Little Brown Jug.'"

"Hey, Prof," a trumpeter said, "we didn't finish that last . . ."

"I said 'LITTLE BROWN JUG!'" Jap screamed at the boy.

The kid almost broke a tooth jamming the mouthpiece back on his lips.

For the third lap Jap called, "'Stars and Stripes Forever!'" Just as the runners passed the bleachers for the final lap he grinned and yelled, "Awright! 'The Gila Monster Fight Song!'"

Jap gradually increased the speed until his band resembled a runaway freight. What the players couldn't see was Billy Gannison crossing the finish line first, his legs pumping like white-skinned piston rods in perfect time with the music. Jap turned at Corley Freemont's ecstatic yell and thumbs up sign.

It was the third lap of the race before Corley finally figured out what Jap was doing. As Jap explained it later, "I saw on his permanent record that Billy'd played trombone in junior high. There's no way you can train an old band player not to stomp his left foot on the strong beat of a march."

"Whyn't ya tell me what you were doin'?" Corley asked.

"Naw, that wouldn'ta worked. It'd get back to Gannison, and he'd see through it and mess up. I had to do a single on this one."

That's why Corley's buying Jap all the coffee he can hold. But Corley's also planning for the future. "Uh, Jasper, you're pretty good with music. You reckon you got any marches or somethin' that'll help that five-seven forward of mine learn to slam dunk?"

Jap grinned and shook his head. "Nah! For that I might have to work with a committee."

Goodie's Scientific Taters

Willard Abbott's boy, Thurgood, just finished his first session in college. Goodie—Thurgood's been called that since he was three days old and slept through the night—enrolled at West Texas Business Ag College over near Breckenridge.

Part of his first year's curriculum included planting a 20×20 plot and writing a paper about the importance of proper business procedures in agriculture.

"Mr. Abbott," the professor said as the session began, "tell us about your project."

Goodie squinted at the two dozen faces focused on him. "I'm thinkin' about doin' some work with potatoes and carrots. My grandma used to . . ."

The professor cut him off. "Thurgood, we've already talked about choosing the proper money crop. Now, if you move to Idaho or down toward the coast you can grow potatoes or turnips or anything you want. Our ground around here is no good for under-the-ground vegetables. You'll need to plant tomatoes or okra or something you know will grow."

"Well, Dr. Dillstaff, I've got a few days before it's time to plant potatoes, so I was plannin' on fixin' the ground like my grandma did it. I can get some . . ."

"Thurgood, this class has a limited time element with a controlled growth period. We start today, and when this class finishes we harvest and eat what we've got."

"I won't plant for at least fifteen days," Goodie said softly. "And my potatoes will be up in plenty of time."

The room quieted. Professor Dillstaff smiled. "Thurgood, you can't get anything up by the time this session is finished if you wait that long. What's the delay?"

"We're just now coming into the full moon. I gotta wait for the dark of the moon to plant potatoes and carrots."

The class erupted in laughter. The professor, normally sympathetic to country boys lost in the labyrinths of double-entry bookkeeping and obscure federal regulations, shook his head and smiled. "Where'd you get those moon phase ideas? From your grandma?"

Goodie blushed, partly from being the center of attention but mostly at the put down of his grandmother. "I'll plant in fifteen days."

For the rest of the class, it was a simple matter of scratching the ground, scattering seeds and pouring on bags of fertilizer. But for Goodie it meant hand-spading the sorriest piece of hard scrabble clay on the school grounds. He hauled in sand and grass clippings and used coffee grounds from the school cafeteria. He hauled out weeds, rocks, and iron-hard clods.

By the end of the first week, the rest of the class was watching the first green shoots work their way through the ground. Goodie hadn't even finished the deep digging. By the time he actually planted his cut potatoes, tomatoes and leaf lettuce waved their sea-green tendrils over the rest of the plots. But from then on, the game was over.

Six weeks later Professor Dillstaff frowned at Goodie's junglelike plot. "Mr. Abbott, this is a controlled experiment. You're only allowed two applications of fertilizer."

"Yes, sir," Goodie said, "I remember, but I decided I didn't need any plastic fertilizer at all. It'll make my expenses-to-profits ratio better."

The professor lifted a luxuriant potato vine thick with blossoms. "I'm having trouble believing you, Thurgood."

"Well, sir, it's the truth. My grandma said if you fix the dirt right and plant your seeds right, you'll get a good crop."

Dillstaff peered closer at a row of delicate leaf lettuce. "What kind of bug killer did you use? Did you know all that insecticide comes out of your dollar allowance?"

"Yes, sir, but all I did was mash up a few of the bugs I found, and added some water, then I sprayed the plants with that. I guess the rest of the bugs didn't like smellin' their dead buddies. At any rate, they left and didn't come back."

"I suppose you got that from . . ."

"Yes sir. From Granny."

The words *good crop* didn't even come close to describing Thurgood Abbott's potato harvest. While the class's above-the-ground crops were puny but acceptable, the few turnips, carrots and onions planted by the others rivaled wallpaper paste for texture and taste. And since Goodie's only expense was a couple of dollars for seed potatoes, his profit ratio ran off the class chart.

Goodie's not much given to bragging—his grandmother took care of that, too—but his daddy, Willard, couldn't help mentioning a call Goodie got his last morning at school from his professor.

"Thurgood, does your, ah, grandmother ever get up here to school?"

"Now and again, yes, sir."

Dillstaff cleared his throat. "Ah, you suppose you might bring her by my classroom, sort of quietly, you understand, so she could explain her theories of moon phase planting. It's, ah, rather quaint."

"I'll see if Grandma can work it into her schedule."

Thurgood Abbott will make it OK through college, if he just doesn't let the professors get in his way. They can be an awful trial.

Not Your Average Send-off

Individualism blooms in the rockiest of soil. The force of circumstances—losing your job, banging your knuckles on a stuck lug nut—may force you to make an unusual decision. But death isn't the normal time to show your nonconformity. That's when you sink back into the expected, into the slot society has designed for you.

Yeah, right.

Delton Cockrell'd been poorly for some time, so when he passed away recently Peggy, his wife, had plenty of opportunity to think about the whole procedure. For a while there, we thought maybe she had a little too much time to think.

Bertie Faye Hogg, our postmistress, cornered Peggy and frowned solicitiously. "I suppose you'll be having the funeral at the Baptist Church. You need any help with arrangements?"

"Thanks for the offer, Bertie Faye," Peggy said. "I'll call."

And she did call Bertie Faye, but it was the next morning and the request wasn't exactly what had been expected. Bertie Faye waddled into the Palace Cafe, a slightly stunned look on her face.

"I can't believe this!" She plopped into the nearest chair. "I'm in charge of the food for Delton's funeral, but all we're having is breakfast stuff."

The chatter ceased. Oliver Greenslope, taking a break from his drugstore, twisted in his chair and frowned. "Whatta ya mean, breakfast stuff?"

"Stuff you eat for breakfast. Peggy's got that funeral set for seven o'clock tomorrow morning, and everybody gets to eat before the service."

"Wait a minute," Eldred Simpson said. "Peggy doesn't have a reservation for that time." Eldred is the pastor for the First Baptist Church. "We've been waiting, but she hasn't called to reserve a time."

"She's got one now." All heads swiveled toward Ornell Whapple walking through the front door.

"You been talking to my church secretary?" Eldred asked.

"Nope. Peggy just walked in down at the Feed & Lumber." He

drew in his breath. "That's where the funeral's gonna be." He paused. "At seven o'clock tomorrow morning we're sayin' good-bye to Delton in my feed store."

The silence of a moon cave descended on the crowd. Gazes shifted from coffee to menus to fleeting touches of other eyes then back to the coffee. It wasn't supposed to be like that. Everybody knows that when you start your final trip from Cedar Gap, your departure lounge is the Baptist church.

"It ain't fittin'," a man said quietly.

"That's for sure," a female voice chimed in. "Really! A feed store!"

"Hey, Yancy. Ain't there some kinda law about havin' a funeral someplace besides a church?"

At that the crowd broke into magpie groups, decrying Peggy's total lack of taste, until Calvin Kinchlow, our eighty-four-year-old Linotype operator at the *Galaxy-Telegraph* suddenly lurched to his feet. Since Cal doesn't do anything suddenly anymore, it caught every eye.

"Now, I'm gonna say this slow," Cal said, "so get it the first time. Where'd Delton spend most of his time when he was in town?"

Heads tilted in thought, and then nodded slowly. Several thumbs jerked in the general direction of the Feed & Lumber.

"And just how many times have you heard Peggy talk about her views on funerals?"

Everybody laughed. Then they shrugged. Peggy's muttered asides at funerals are part of the Cedar Gap folklore: "Everybody lines up in a place that looks like a bank lobby and smells like a greenhouse to smile at a cadaver in a fancy foot locker and lie about how good he looks."

That's when the whole Palace Cafe crowd relaxed and grinned. "If people can get married in a helicopter or a cave," Yancy McWhirter said, "why can't people get buried from a feed store?"

It was as relaxed a funeral as anybody could remember. A hundred or so people meandered in just after sunup; picked up a plate of eggs, sausage, hash browns and coffee; and then sat around on feed sacks and bales of hay remembering "that time when ol' Delton mistook that mule for . . ." or "when me 'n Del was off fishin' and saw that coyote that . . ."

Of course, Eldred Simpson had on his marrying/burying blue suit, so when he got the bit in his teeth and talked too long, all the kids got restless. It was either wiggle or die. But by the time Bertie Faye had stirred up some Kool-Aid, Peggy already had the kids outside teaching them Red Rover with a tennis ball. Like she said, "Life's for the living. Delton knew that."

That's why nobody's looking overly dejected right now. They hadn't been to a funeral. It was just a bon voyage party, except with a strong smell of oat straw.

SATURDAY'S JOURNAL

VISITOR FROM THE PLANET

NEW YORK

ell, it's Saturday, and our visitor is gone from Cedar Gap. It wasn't much of a visit, actually more of a drop-in.

Thursday morning Milo Shively came busting through the door of the Palace Cafe yelling, "A private jet from New York City's landin' at our airport!"

Salt shakers tipped and chairs fell over as everyone jumped to be the first one to the airport. The group arrived just as a sleek propjet dipped onto the far end of the runway, and then drifted to a stop at the single hangar.

A slim, elegant man in an Italian-cut pinstripe suit emerged and straightened his tie. He surveyed the crowd disdainfully from the top step of the jet. Then he approached them slowly.

"Howdy," Milo said, sticking out his hand. "Welcome to Cedar Gap. Can we help ya?"

One eyebrow raised as the man took a deep breath and said, "By dabe is Dortid Bidsbad. I wad to red a car."

Confused glances bounced back and forth as lips tried to recreate the strange syllables from the polished and elegant stranger. The man spread his hands in frustration, and then handed Milo a card.

"Ooooooh!" Milo said. "This here's Mr. Norton Minsman, from the firm of Minsman and Wimsley."

"Wobsley," the man corrected. "Bidsbad ad Wobsley. As I said, I deed to red ad autobobile. Is there a reddal agedcy here?"

Milo peered at the man's mouth, trying heroically to mimic the lip movement. "Oh! You need to rent a car!" He turned to the crowd. "Uh, lessee. Lester, don't you still have that ol' brown '79 Merc with the rusty door? You'd rent that, wouldn't ya?"

"Aw, sure," Lester Goodrich said. "If Mr. Minsman only needs it for a day or two he can just borry it."

Minsman frowned. "Do," he said, shaking his head, "I'll pay. I deed to drive aroud the area a bid." He snorted in a futile attempt to get past a totally stopped up nose. "By firb is lookig at sob farblad aroud here."

Twenty bodies leaned in toward the man as twenty pairs of lips worked over the incoherent blobs of sound. "Did he say somethin' about farmland?" Lester whispered.

"Ride!" the man said. "We thig your area would be good for growig a dew tybe of wadderbellod sob peoble id Fradce develobed. We're tryig to red sob farblad."

Murphy Gumpton squinched his face. "I'm gettin' a headache. Did he say watermelons?"

"*Ride!* Wadderbellods. We deed a lod of saddy soil. We heard you had . . ."

Everyone shrugged sadly. "Naw," Ferrell Epperson said. "There's nothin' but red clay and caliche around here."

Minsman frowned. "By agedt specifigly listed Cedar Gab."

"He probably got us mixed up with Cedar Creek over 'round Nacogdoches."

Minsman's face fell. "I cad believe it! Baybe thad's the blace." He turned to go. "Zorry to hab bothered you."

"Hey, well, listen, Mr. Minsman, you can't leave hungry. We got a great brisket workin' over at the Palace Cafe. Our treat!"

Minsman sighed and let himself be led to the cafe where IdaLou Vanderburg squinted at his order of "sob ob thad barbecue Bister Ebbersod recobbedded."

IdaLou nodded slowly, muttered "Uh huh," and then walked back in the cafe's storage room and picked six tiny red peppers off a dried bush hanging behind the door. She ground them up in a plate of her best barbeque before sliding it in front of the dapper visitor.

Minsman was on his third bite before the caustic spice started clawing at every pore in his head. He sucked in air, huffed it out, and began snorting. Suddenly his eyes flew open as he grunted—and air actually went out through his nose.

"My nose! What's happening to—wait a minute, I said *nose*. That word's got an *n* in it. Nose! Minsman! Minsman and Wombsley. Hey, nonny nonny." He vaulted to his feet. "Listen! I said, 'Hey, nonny nonny!' "

Ferrell spread his hands. "So? How long you had that cold?"

"Eighteen years," Minsman said.

They bundled Snortin' Norton back into his jet and waved him on his way. As Stafford Higginbotham said, "Actually, I kinda liked the way he talked before he ate. Made me think we had a Finn or Ay-rab or somethin' foreign right here in town."

"Reckon they could get IdaLou for practicin' medicine without a license?" Milo asked, sipping his coffee.

Stafford shrugged. "They better not try it with IdaLou. She'll get a hoe handle and put Minsman's nose back the way it was."

And peppers won't clear that up.

CHAPTER 6

CORLEY FREEMONT:

SATURDAY'S WARRIOR

The Only Seven-footer in Gap History

Saturdays turn up every seven days or so in most places, but Corley Freemont, the coach of everything played with a ball down at South Taylor County Junior College, swears that in the fall there's a maximum of sixteen hours from Saturday to Saturday. There's never enough time for practice or healing between football or basketball games.

Corley runs his STCJC athletic program on a pretty short financial leash. Since he can't give scholarships he has to rely on personal persuasion, plus some underground alumni help, to snare even modest talent for his Fighting Gila Monster teams. When he finally does run into a decent prospect, he tends to hyperventilate.

"Now, Son," Corley said, grinning maniacally. "We got us a tradition of instillin' a fightin' spirit in our players, somethin' that'll help ya throughout your life." Corley was staring straight into the belt buckle of Mephistopheles Jefferson, the only seven-foot basketball player he'd ever seen up close. "We teach winnin' attitude. We teach desire. We teach not givin' up till the fat lady sings."

"Yes, sir," Mephistopheles said quietly, gazing down at the wispy bald spot on Corley's blocky head. "But I'm getting sort of tired of basketball."

Corley's blood froze. "Aw, no, Son! Ya gotta keep the faith. The game a basketball's like the game a life. If you're given a couple a steps head start, like bein' taller than most of the trees in this town, then you can help a lot a people." Corley frowned. "Where'd you go to school that I never heard a you?"

The bony shoulders shrugged. "Eight schools in the last six years. My father's in the military and I've been on teams all over the world."

"Awright, yeah, I can understand that." Corley's eyes began to glimmer. "Yeah, uh, yeah, that's good. You'll make a great Gila Monster."

"Uh, Mr. Freemont, I'll only have a little free time, and . . ."

"There's no problem there, son. None atall." Corley bounced around like a demented dwarf. "We'll work classes around practice." What Corley meant was that he'd work everything around whatever got in the way, including the Second Coming. Corley knew that in the Bigs they would call this kind of talent "The Franchise." Mephistopheles Jefferson would make the difference.

Boy, howdy, would he!

Of the eight boys on this year's team, the tallest is only six-two. When Mephistopheles walked in for the first practice, all talking ceased.

"That first scrimmage was closer to a waltz than a basketball game," Corley said. "I guess they were intimidated. It was the first time they ever got cricks in their necks playing basketball." He shook his head sadly. "But that only lasted one day. By the second practice they were elbowing and shoving Mephistopheles all over the gym. It was beautiful!"

The fact that Mephistopheles Jefferson only carried 135 pounds on his seven-foot frame made him look like a cadaverous xylophone turned up on one end. His lack of muscle allowed guards a foot and a half shorter to push him out of the free throw circle. But when he finally got the ball he drove to the basket like Patton crossing the Rhine.

"You could stop him, but it would have taken a 2 × 4 or a hand grenade." Corley sucked in a deep breath. "Nobody, I'm talkin' *nobody*, in our conference coulda touched us. I was starin' a league championship straight in the eyes."

"Whatta ya mean, 'was'?" somebody asked. "Ya didn't let him get away, didja, Corley?"

Corley sighed as he gazed forlornly out the window. "Aw, it was a combination a things. He just needed to be somewhere's else." He frowned, the pain evident. "Well, I gotta get back to the gym."

Everyone looked around, wondering at Corley's letting a sure thing slip through his fingers. Then Wilson Kruddmeier, our county auditor, set his coffee mug down carefully and cleared his throat.

"I hope this isn't privileged information, but Rose Trundle, the secretary down at the college, told me Corley's the one who sent Mephistopheles Jefferson packing."

Jaws dropped, heads swiveled. "Naw!" "Cain't be!" "Throw out a seven-footer? Serious up, Wilson."

Wilson nodded. "Corley saw that Mephistopheles was a tall, skinny stack of unhappy, so he looked up the boy's transcript. He couldn't believe the recommendation letters he found."

"So?" Yancy McWhirter said. "What'd they say?"

"That the kid's a pure mathematics genius. But he was too shy to apply anyplace but at a little school like ours." Wilson motioned for more coffee to lubricate his memory. "Anyway, Corley quietly called an engineer friend of his, the friend called M.I.T., and the kid got a full math scholarship. As far as the Gila Monsters go, he's history."

"And so's the championship," Yancy muttered. Then he smiled, and so did everyone else. Everybody in the Palace Cafe knew Corley had lost a championship, but he'd won a kid.

And a town.

Seems like a fair enough trade.

By the Dawn's Early Sweat

Although Corley has lost his share of ball games, track meets, and other contests over the years he's been at STCJC, he tends to shuck those like a duck sheds water. As he says, "Ya cain't look back. Some-

thin' may be gainin' on ya." That's probably the reason those occasional wins pump his adrenalin so. When he does finally see a win-
ning score after the last buzzer, his latent ego and transcendent
confidence rebounds like a superball in a dryer.

That's not always good.

One Thursday afternoon, Mabel Southfall, the elementary school
principal, walked in the Palace Cafe looking more haggard than
usual.

"Hey, Mable, you look worse than caliche concrete," somebody
said. "Your cat run off again?"

"Worse," she muttered. "I could get another cat. What I need is a
substitute for our first-grade class tomorrow morning, and there's
not a soul available between the Trinity and the Pecos."

Corley, whose Fighting Gila Monster basketball team had squeaked
out a win the night before, gazed out the window. He turned to
Mabel. "When do those kiddoes in first grade get out?'

"Two-thirty," Mabel said. "Why?"

"Aw, I was just thinkin'. We got a game tomorrow night so I
cancelled early practice." Corley shrugged. "I suppose I could take
the class for ya."

Mabel gazed at Corley. "You've never had any elementary experience, have you? There's twenty-two of those little kids, you know."

Corley waved his hand to dismiss the problem. "Hey, I run thirty
or so on my football team. I mean, how tough can it be teachin'
three plus three?"

"You're serious!"

"Of course, I am! My degree's in education, same as your'n."

Mabel nodded slowly, counting her options. The list was extremely short. "Well, all right. My back's to the wall." She sighed.
"Children start arriving at eight o'clock. When do you want to pick
up the teacher's lesson plans?"

"Aaaaaah, I'll just come in a few minutes early. I mean, we're
talkin', what, six-year-olds?"

Mable shook her head as she backed toward the door. "Right."
She started to say something else, but then she nodded. "OK.
They're in Room 4 at the end of the hall." She turned quickly and
left before either one of them could back out.

"Listen, Corley," Vera Frudenburg, our third-grade teacher, said. "It's an old rule that the lower the grade, the harder the teaching." Corley looked disgusted. His leadership was being called into question. "Now, come on, Vera. I remember my own first grade like it was yesterday. Besides, it's only one day."

Corley walked in the first grade room the next morning at seven-thirty, poured some coffee from his Thermos into its plastic cap, and then bent over the teacher's lesson plan book already opened to the day.

"Hmmm," he muttered. 'Reading book, chapter 3 for the B group, chapter 4 for the A group.' Sounds about right. And . . . 'adding and subtracting 6's.' " He nodded again. "And . . . 'lesson on electricity in science book.' " He spread his hands, shrugged and smiled. "Piece a cake. I may quit this college stuff and just teach elemen . . . " Then his eyes spied the next line:

"Second hour."

He gagged on his coffee. "Wait a minute. I thought that was the whole day." He ran quickly down the next listing: "Spelling, social studies, drug abuse education," which was followed by the terrifying line: "Third hour."

Beads of sweat formed on his upper lip as he hurriedly screwed the still-full top back on his Thermos and grabbed for the foot-high stack of books just as five children and two confused and frowning mothers walked through the door, thirty minutes early.

Corley was still flapping wildly through teacher's manuals when the last kid dropped into a chair. He struggled to control his voice as he faced twenty-two six-year-olds.

"Uhhhhh, . . . I'm Mr. Freemont, your teacher today." He swallowed hard. "We'll start with, aaaaaah, reading, . . . yeah, reading. Then we'll, . . . uhhhhh, . . . " He saw a waving hand. "Yeah, what is it, kid?"

A tremulous voice piped, "Teacher, aren't we gonna do our opening exercises?"

"Oh. Sure! Great idea." Finally, something in his area of expertise. "OK, all y'all line up here in three lines, tall ones in the back." The children looked around, baffled. "Come on, now, move it, move it, move it!"

The children shoved chairs aside and shuffled into three lines.

"OK, now, jumpin' jacks! Ever'body, hup—tyup, hup—tyup, hup—tyup. Come on, kid, get those legs pumpin' or we'll do five laps around this whole school. Aw'right, now down on the floor for some situps. Hook those feet under those little chairs and let's raise some sweat. Uuuuuuup! Back! Uuuuuuup! Back!"

It was on the squat-straddles that the boys' enthusiasm kicked in like an afterburner. Halfway through the shadow boxing the girls' adrenalin overcame their mystification. The noise level approached that of a jet at takeoff just as Mabel Southfall walked in with the list of announcements for the real opening exercises.

But by this time the kids were wired. Corley couldn't have aimed their learning experience with a cannon. Besides their attention span being measured in microseconds, the students discovered that Mr. Freemont was never quite sure just who had gone to the bathroom. Consequently, each was excused something over twenty-nine times before lunch.

As Mabel summed it up, "Actually, it wasn't all that bad for the kids. Their motor skills improved markedly, they learned to simplify all their questions, and they now know at least three different ways to spell *February*. Corley's the one we ought to worry about."

And that's the truth. The whole next day he sat by himself off in the corner, glaring out the Palace Cafe window. Every time a little kid walked by, he slid under the table.

SATURDAY'S JOURNAL

MOVING DAY

 ell, it's Saturday again in Cedar Gap, and the Whitlocks just left, their Ryder van pulling away like a yellow elephant lumbering off to die.

A month or so ago Darrell Whitlock's job just disappeared. He's worked for a national firm up in Abilene for most of his adult life, supervising a small assembly line. But within the last year his firm found it could import the individual pieces semifinished cheaper than Darrell's assembly line could provide them.

"My people came up with every innovation known to modern mechanics," Darrell said over a cup of Palace Cafe coffee, "but nothing could make up the difference in price. We even invented some new machines, but nothing was enough."

Eve and Darrell Whitlock took a long look at their future and the Cedar Gap situation. Then, reluctantly, they took his firm's offer to relocate in Syracuse, New York. The decision was a tough one, and a long time coming.

"You any idea how much snow those people get in Syracuse?" Darrell's eyes glazed over at the thought. "I called the preacher at the church we'll probably attend, and he said last year was a mild winter—they only got about a hundred inches. I'm gonna die!"

"Naw, Darrell, you'll do fine," Russell Underwood said. "You can go ice skating and skiing and fish through the ice."

"OK, Russ, I'll be expecting you in January. You and me'll go sit in a forty-below-zero wind chill and do some big time ice fishing."

"Uh, well," Russ stammered. "Actually, my septic system business gets real busy about that time, so I'd better make it July or August."

Darrell just nodded. "Ya know, I never thought I'd be nostalgic about a 102-degree day, but right now it sounds pretty good." Then he smiled. "But they've got some good Russian and Korean restaurants, so we won't starve."

"Forget that Commie stuff. How's the barbecue up north?"

Darrell sighed and waited a long time to answer. "Now, that's gonna be a problem. About all they got is pig barbecue and Polish sausage."

Eyes squinted in disbelief. Finally Edgar Allen Plymate said, "No brisket?"

"Nope. And no mesquite for decent coals, either."

"Those people are barbarians!" "I never figured on you havin' to camp out like that." "Can they read 'n write?"

"Come on, now, people!" Eve exclaimed. "They got other things to make up for Cedar Gap barbecued brisket."

"Like what?"

When Eve hesitated, somebody yelled, "Like Darrell and Eve."

A big round of applause caused both of them to redden and grin. Everybody knew it was time to leave. Darrell pushed his chair back, then stood quietly. "Look, um, I'm not much for speeches, either giving or listening." He waited through some good-natured bantering and light applause. "So I'll just say that we'll miss this place something terrible, but we'll get back occasionally, and . . . y'all come see us, ya hear?"

The whole Palace Cafe crowd walked them to the moving van. Brenda Beth gave each of the kids a Dr Pepper. "That's so's you'll have to stop at least ten times before you leave Texas." Amid the laughter, Eve dabbed at her eyes. Darrell cleared his throat. The truck's gears ground, the motor raced, and the Whitlocks eased away from the Palace Cafe and our lives.

"I'll send 'em the first mesquite sprig I see next March."

"Maybe we could take up a collection and ship 'em a whole cord of split mesquite."

"And Dolly can put them on the mailing list for the *Galaxy-Telegraph* so's they can keep up with the real world."

But we all knew we would do none of those things. Cedar Gap is one world; Eve and Darrell are going to another. Eventually the pain will soften and their memories will take on a mythic glow like a half-remembered lullaby your mother sang. On a cool day in July, Eve and Darrell will sip some coffee and wonder how they ever stood anything above eighty-five degrees.

Then from somewhere a snippet of country-western music will drift over their fence as a funny little twist of wind-blown dust curls into a sand devil. Or a red and orange sunset will paint their white house the color of a marigold. Or one of their children will say, "I sure wish we had some good barbecue."

And they'll remember how they stood it.

It was no problem at all.

CHAPTER 7

MUSIC AT THE GAP

Give My Regards to Cedar Gap, *A Musical*

couple of months ago our Cedar Gap Floral Artistry Club figured they'd peaked out as far as the visual aspects of Cedar Gap front yards were concerned. The club members—nine hyperactive women and two reluctant husbands—frowned at the union list of herb and cactus gardens in town. It was unanimously decided the time had come to conquer another art form.

Ora Barstow patted her tightly pinned bun. "We could break some new artistic ground by sponsoring a performance of a Broadway musical. Cedar Gap's always been known for its fine musicianship."

It was an idea whose time had come. The women chattered like guinea hens as they divvied up the committee assignments. They were quick to learn that as long as the festival lived in the abstract it was a world-shattering success; it was when the nitty-gritty of particulars surfaced that the clod fell into the churn.

It was decided that, because of tender egos and spotty memories, the members of the CGFAC should limit themselves to singing in the chorus. Soloists would come from that huge pool of natural talent called Greater Metropolitan Cedar Gap. And despite the gene-deep animosity for that other state north of here, the musical would be *Oklahoma*!

There were, of course, the traditional tryout problems of telling someone who's fifty-one that she can't play the ingenue of twenty-one. But finally the casting was complete, with the primary musical problem being balancing a chorus of seventeen women and four men, three of the latter having severe rhythmic problems when walking and chewing gum at the same time. The chorus could either move or sing, but not both simultaneously.

"Now, look, Silas," Murphy Gumpton puffed, "ya get either my foot or my throat. Pick one."

Silas Eddardson, the professor at the Cedar Gap Conservatory of Music, laid down his three-foot-long baton. "Mr. Gumpton, I'm relatively sure that Messers Rodgers and Hammerstein had some kind of brisk activity in mind when they wrote in the score 'All Dance.' Now, once again, from the top."

The Cowboys' Chorus took on the tonal resonance of a '37 Ferguson tractor with a bad plug and no muffler. "Oh, the"—stomp, stomp—"farmer and the"—forward, back—"cowman should be"—twirl one way or the other—"friends"—pant heavily.

Since the five members of Cody Cuttshaw's Side B Band were the only instrumentalists in town, they got the nod as the pit orchestra. Probably the aforementioned Hammerstein and Rodgers never anticipated loud speakers capable of frying bacon. Silas, his eyes squinted against the jetlike roar, vainly waved off the machine-gunning drummer.

The single performance in the elementary school cafetorium was a sellout. Whereas the room usually featured parents and grandparents watching kids perform, now it was kids and grandkids grinning and pointing at middle-aged relatives huffing and gasping through choreographic niceties.

The whole evening was a astonishing success, and a great warmup for . . .

The All-Star Gap Chorus

Every other year, a committee is organized to plan the Biennial Cedar Gap Elementary School Homecoming for the old grads. Along
with the traditional dance, the Guess-Who-These-Are picture display
and the We're-Truly-Surprised-You-Succeeded awards, the steering
committee decided an all-star chorus would set a properly classy tone
to match its graduates. Since it was homecoming, they thought it
would be nice if a former student directed.

Forming the chorus was simple; if you'd ever sung in the Cedar
Gap Elementary Chorus you were eligible, which meant everybody
who'd ever attended school in Cedar Gap. The word went out for
interested singers to meet at the school auditorium on Tuesday
night.

Aurally, that first chorus meeting resembled feeding time at the
zoo. Prospective conductors scribbled their names on the chalk-
board, and then took turns learning to follow the singers.

Murphy Gumpton sings bass in the Baptist church choir where he
takes all the solos that aren't over five notes high or eight beats long.
More than that and he tends toward bug-eyed hyperventilation. "I
can handle that solo in "Bridge over Troubled Water" just fine. All
we'll have to do is trim some high notes and add two commas."

Oliver Greenslope, designated follower of the moment, shushed
Murph. "It's a tenor solo."

"Well, then, just lower the whole piece."

Corinne Iverson, the fill-in pianist at the Cedar Gap Rotary Club,
blanched to the color of a hospital sheet. "Oliver, I'm only accom-
panying with one hand right now. You get fancy and you'll be conducting a cappella."

The second conductor, Cody Cuttshaw, mentioned his extensive
experience with the Side B Band, his little five-member country-
western group. "Listen, I'm the only trained and currently practicing
professional musician in this town. We're gonna pick up the—yeah,
Toad, put your drums over there by the piano—pick up the "Hallelujah Chorus" just a tad. Corinne, take it from the top. One . . .
two . . . one, two, three, four."

Cody might have made it except for the bongos on "And he shall reign for ever and ever."

But then somebody said it wasn't right for anybody but Miss Beatrice to conduct.

"Ain't she up in Denver with a sick sister?"

"She was, but some of us were afraid this would happen, so we pitched in and bought her a ticket home. She just walked in."

A tremendous wave of applause welcomed a smallish, bright-eyed woman in her eighties. Miss Beatrice—which is pronounced Be-AT-russ—Bedford stalked on stage and grabbed the baton. "All right, straighten those lines and get your heads up." From then on it was a *rehearsal*. There was none of that lifted-pinkie nicety to her conducting method. Downbeats resembled a General Motors punch press. Cues sizzled with the exactitude of laser beams.

They really didn't need a concert; everybody heard Miss Beatrice was directing and ran over for the rehearsal. "Makes Georg Solti look arthritic," was the way Edgar Allen Plymate described Miss Beatrice's conducting style. "Sort of a combination of Leonard Bernstein and Crocodile Dundee."

Last night the three-number concert was a fantastic success. Cody got to perform the "Hallelujah Chorus" trumpet part on his electric guitar, and he even turned down the reverb. Ambrosio Gonzales worked up a mariachi-rap version of the solo on "Bridge over Troubled Water." And the Tuscola High School shop class provided a spectacular brake-drum-and-crowbar finale for Verdi's "Anvil Chorus." Miss Beatrice was called back for three curtain calls.

Later, Stafford Higginbotham looked up from tidying some stacks of music when Miss Beatrice walked by. "Lady, where'd you learn to conduct like that? You didn't do that with us kids in school."

Miss Beatrice Bedford wiped her forehead. "You'd laugh."

"Nah, I won't."

"Kung fu movies on cable."

Hig let out a roar. "I can't believe it! Bruce Lee taught you conducting?"

"Better than that," Miss Beatrice said, glancing around. "Chuck Norris. Bruce never took on more than twenty or thirty. Chuck always has at least a hundred." She nodded at the chattering singers milling around the stage. "I figure that bunch is just about equal to a platoon of machinegun-carrying Cambodian rebels." Her face squinched up. "Except the Cambodians would probably sing better in tune."

But they'd never love you like that chorus. Some things are better than accuracy.

That Marvelous Christmas Pageant

For several Decembers, all thirty-nine or so members of the Cedar Gap Independent Full-Gospel Non-Denominational Four-Square Missionarian Church of the Apostolic Believers have staged a simulation of those midwinter events of two thousand years ago. Up until now they've been fairly simple affairs—a piano flourish, some familiar seasonal hymns stuck in among sheet-covered children gazing at a doll on a bale of hay, and a grand finale by the nine-member choir singing the "Hallelujah Chorus." That was followed by spiced cider and homemade cookies in the Fellowship Hall, which is known locally as the Big Classroom. It was a nice hour.

"But not this year!" Pastor T. Edsel Pedigrew trumpeted. "This whole Christmas season is about courage, and that's what we'll show this town. This time around we're gonna put a hundred people in our pageant. We'll tell that ancient story in all its ancient glory," a bit of doggerel provided by Delmarine, T. Edsel's lumpish wife.

From the beginning it was obvious that logistics would be the main frog in the dumplings. T. Edsel squinted at the tiny stage area at the front of the sanctuary.

"Now, Honey, if all the angels go up there, we'll never have space for even the manger, much less the animals."

Delmarine surveyed the sanctuary like Moses stumbling onto the Red Sea. "Ambrosio's due here any minute and he can . . . there he is! Ambrosio, explain about the Angel Choir."

Ambrosio Gonzales, our local intuitive mechanic, had reworked some old leather harness into shoulder straps that allowed the entire choir to angle off the right side of the pulpit area on three levels like a Renaissance altar painting.

"And Sister Oliphant has volunteered to dress the Angel Choir and make some crowns out of aluminum foil."

It quickly became obvious that, with a total church membership of thirty-nine, volunteers or conscripts were desperately needed. For ten days before the pageant every living soul, fearful of being transformed into a shepherd or a wise man, dodged into a doorway or an alley anytime T. Edsel or Delmarine set foot on Main Street.

The night of the Christmas pageant carried the electricity of history in the making. Two hundred surviving Main Street dodgers lined the walls and crowded ten deep into pews designed for eight adults. Many held kids on their laps.

With a grandiloquent crash, the pianist rattled a brave but futile trumpet fanfare imitation, and the show was on. Overall it was a great success, primarily because everybody knew everybody else and was properly impressed either that the neighbor could indeed hit a near relative of that high note in "O Holy Night" or that someone known for clenched-jaw sobriety could stand there in a bathrobe and declaim solemnly, "I am come from a far-removed land following that there yon star."

Finally, the concluding manger scene was due, and everyone, muscles long since atrophied from sitting packed like birdshot in a 12-gauge shell, bent forward expectantly. What they couldn't know was that the Baby Jesus this particular year was the prophetically named Jesus Maria Rolando Luis Gonzales, Ambrosio's fifth and loudest young'un.

For two solid hours Jesus Maria had been squirming in the arms of a string of tired Gonzales relatives, awaiting his moment in the spotlight. Jesus Maria had also been sucking noisily at a totally unrewarding pacifier. The kid needed food in the worst kind of way. By the time his cue finally came he was gnawing the nap off his blanket.

Since both religious history and Near East archaeology are silent about the presence of a pacifier in the manger, Sister Oliphant gracelessly plucked the pacifier out of Jesus Maria's mouth just as she shoved Mary and Joseph and said, "You're on!"

It was Ambrosio's unfortunate job to be caravansary manager on this particular pageant. As such, he was holding the halters of the mule and two goats just as Jesus Maria let out a scream that had to be heard in Guadalajara. Each goat, assuming that the other was being mutilated, butted the mule in an unseemly place, causing the mule to bray and lash out with both rear feet. The piano, never a staunch piece of equipment even in its ancient heyday, caught both hooves square in the middle octave. The pianist screamed as the entire instrument toppled onto a cage, releasing four indignant ducks.

T. Edsel hissed to the choir director to sing the "Hallelujah Chorus" a cappella, which they attempted, but the confused conductor got it too high. When the lone tenor came in on "And Heeeeeeee shall reign forever and ever," it sounded less like music and more like the cotton gin letting out on Friday.

Somebody, we don't know who, managed to start "Joy to the World." The assembly sang not wisely but well, and the pageant was over.

As Dolly Hooter said when somebody asked for her critique of the play, "*Great*'s not the word."

Le Conservatoire d'Cedar Gap

The Annual Recital is about due. We know because the parade of young'uns toting banjos and accordions and trumpets and snare drums has begun. Most Saturdays it starts about eight o'clock; this year, according to Brenda Beth Kollwood, our Palace Cafe waitress, it began at sunup, and the kids are coming in bunches.

About fifteen years ago Silas Eddardson moved to town to open the Cedar Gap Conservatory of Music in a renovated shed behind his house. A sprang-haired angular water bird of a man, Professor Eddardson's clothes run to greenish tweed year-round. His vocabulary tends toward the baroque.

If there's one word to describe Silas's musical talents, it's *versatile*. He teaches everything. If you scrape across it, pick at it or aggress upon it, then Professor Eddardson teaches it. Somebody asked him how he could learn fifteen or twenty instruments.

"Now, really, dear friend, the musical arts are all interrelated. If you learn piano, then of course a musician with even minimal attainments can play organ, accordion, or even harpsichord. Study clarinet, and flute or saxophone is simple." Silas seemed a bit miffed that he would be questioned.

It's not that Sy is a great artist. Actually, no one has ever heard a single note from him in a concert. "I am a pedagogue, a facilitator of culture in this Saharan musical landscape." Normally taciturn and aloof, Silas turns into a slavering carnivore when discussing Cedar Gap's bleak musical vistas. "When the height of a town's culture is epitomized by the collected oeuvre of gentlemen named Hank, Merle"—he pauses, his face twisted—"and Willie, then can the demise of civilization be far in arrears?"

Some are a bit confused at Professor Eddardson's style. "I can handle the music," Corinne Iverson said. "It's his announcements that concern me. You remember last year he announced the Götterdämmerung music of Wagner, and we couldn't figure if he was clearing his throat or cussing."

Eleven months out of the year Silas slouches around, grousing gently about lost music, dented horns or the spiritual deprivation evident in halftime shows. But to his students he is kindness incarnate.

Then, the month before the annual recital, Silas sloughs off his mortal skin of the laconic mentor and turns into Professor Eddardson, the Final Barrier to Total Barbaric Abandonment.

"Benjamin, a Buddhist knows the sound of one hand clapping, and now I've learned from you the sound of one lip playing trombone."

"Miss Breedlow, I refuse to believe Mr. Stradivarius would design an instrument whose strings would sound better if placed back in the cat."

"All right, we'll try the democratic approach. Hands up, all those in favor of the key of E-flat."

The Cedar Gap Conservatory of Music Annual Recital—a highlight of our crowded social calendar—began at seven o'clock and ended about five hours later at eight o'clock. Mysterious black cases disgorged buffed and polished instruments that caught the light like gemstones. Scrubbed faces glowed above buttoned collars that had long-since been outgrown.

The curtain-raising accordion duet playing Rimsky-Korsakov's "Capriccio Espagnol" was followed by Berlioz's "March to the Scaffold" arranged for bass saxophone, autoharp, and snares. There was even a vocal quartet doing the tomb scene from *Aida*.

But the piece of resistance was the entire Ensemble de Conservatoire performing Tchaikovsky's "1812 Overture" complete with shotguns firing blanks into empty steel barrels for the substitute cannons.

Today Sy ambled into the Palace Cafe and ordered some coffee. He looked haggard and bone weary, but serene. After the annual recital everybody takes two weeks off. We congratulated him for a great concert. Then, since we knew the echoes of masterworks die slowly, we left him alone to mend.

Three of his students ran in for some Dr Peppers, then spied their musical guru. They bounced around him, chattering like mockingbirds. Presently, music forgotten, they ran out again. Sy sat very quietly, staring into his coffee. Then he smiled, slowly, fully.

One of the kids, a red-haired, runty boy, skittered back in for a doughnut. Somebody cornered the boy and asked him why Professor Eddardson was smiling. The boy frowned. "I dunno. Maybe it's something we said."

"What did you say to him?"

The boy shrugged. "Nothin'. Just that we liked him." The boy turned to go. Then he stopped. "And we told him he made us want to be better players."

We nodded. Now *that* would look nice on a tombstone.

SATURDAY'S JOURNAL

T. EDSEL PEDIGREW, PH.D.,

UPS, PDQ

Well, it's another Saturday here in Cedar Gap, and down at the Independent Full Gospel Non-Denominational Four Square Missionarian Church of the Apostolic Believers the consensus is that scholarship is fine, but heresy by mail must be considered downright faith-threatening.

Several days ago, Pastor T. Edsel Pedigrew sat relaxed with the newest issue of *The Missionarian Rebuttal*, the biweekly tabloid of who went where, which pulpits are polluted, and how many came forward in Missionarian congregations. A two-inch ad caught his eye.

"No Time For A Doctorate? Sure You Do! Get a Ph.D. by Mail. We Give Credit for Life's Experiences!!"

T. Edsel squinted at the address: Graduate School of Divinity, Our Lady of Mucky Swamp University, Miami, Florida.

"Delmarine!" he yelled. "I think maybe my grad school problems are solved!"

Early the next day he phoned the 800 number.

"Divinity school." The silken voice was compassion incarnate. "This is Dean Hermon. Can we help you?"

"Yes. This is Pastor T. Edsel Pedigrew in Cedar Gap, Texas. I'm interested in your doctoral program."

"Excellent, Pastor Pedigrew!" Dean Hermon gushed. "No doubt you're considering our Accelerated Program for Established Religionists."

"Sounds good. It sounded like your ad said you give credit for things I already know."

"Of course, of course! As an example, no doubt you have solved many problems in your church, such as working on classroom allocation, teacher training, and possibly even parking."

"Aw, you betcha! Hundreds a times."

"Well, then," Dean Hermon said smoothly, "you would qualify perfectly for our Seminar on Crowd Control. And how about directing the choir? That requires a great deal of both judgment and physical activity, does it not?"

"Well, yeah," T. Edsel said slowly. He remembered the most recent out-of-control Christmas pageant.

"Marvelous! Then you have all of the prerequisites for our athletic scholarship. What else of a physical nature have you engaged in for the benefit of your congregation?"

"Ummm, well, I replanted three trees by the side door after Sister Oliphant's brakes gave out."

"Well, there you are, Pastor Pedigrew! That qualifies for our Botany Colloquium, and if you could prepare a thorough one-page description of your Sister Oliphant's reaction to destroying the trees we could probably do a Guided Study in Abnormal Behavior for advanced credit."

"Hey, this is soundin' good! Now, what kinda class work we talking about?"

"Pastor Pedigrew, we are an accredited institution. We have very high standards! First, you list all of your abilities. From that, we very carefully prepare your degree plan. Finally, for your graduation document you will be required to do a research paper listing at least thirty religious words in the dictionary of your choice, with your prayerful annotations about your own denomination's particular views of those words." Dean Hermon hesitated. His voice dropped an octave. "You are a Spirit-filled pastor, are you not?"

"Oh, absolutely!" T. Edsel could tell from the way Dean Hermon said it that *Spirit* was capitalized.

"*Wonnnnnnderful!* Then I'll just have my secretary send you our application packet with complete information, plus an engraved copy of our school hymn and our fight song, 'Divinity, Divanity, Divonity Fudge.' Now, Pastor Pedigrew, what denomination do you serve?"

"I'm with the Texas Independent Branch of the Apostolic Brethren."

"Aaaaaaah . . . yeeees. I believe one of our recent graduates was affiliated with your Apostolic Brethren. From Oklahoma, as I recall."

T. Edsel's mind froze. "Wait a minute. That wouldn't be from up around Stincher City, Oklahoma, would it?"

"You know, I believe it was!"

"What was his name?"

"Oh, dear, let me see. Wingle, Wangle, something like . . ."

T. Edsel snorted. "Delius Wongle from Stincher City?"

"That's it! You know him?"

"Know him? I reckon I know that man. Stincher City's the head-quarters for the Anti-Missionarians who've been preachin' against us Missionarians for more years than I've been alive. I'm sorry, Dean, but any school that'd recognize Wongle's work, well, there's just no way I could ever hang its diploma on my wall."

"Now, Pastor Pedigrew, possibly we could . . ."

But T. Edsel had already hung up. As he said later over a cup of coffee, "An education is good to have. But heresy's a whole 'nother thing."

Oliver Greenslope nodded. "Sorry to hear about that, Edsel. I guess that shelves your doctoral plans for awhile."

"Well, naw," T. Edsel said. "I got a call in to the Church of the Holy Knowly Graduate University, over around Shreveport. They got an extension plan where I can phone in all of my scholarly work." He nodded slowly. "And they never heard of Stincher City. I just feel cleaner that way."

CHAPTER 8

THOSE OLD DUDES

ancy McWhirter sat stirring his cup of Palace Cafe coffee, his head tilted back to focus his bifocals on the *Galaxy-Telegraph*. "Ya know, the problem with gettin' older, is that everything reminds you of something else. I was lookin' at these pictures of former U.S. presidents, and I thought for sure it was the Farm Bureau down at Tuscola."

IdaLou Vanderburg, our chief cafe cook, frowned at the front-page picture. "Just lookit those old dudes. I know at least three people from right around here who look like Gerald Ford, and one of them's Eugenia May Danciger." She squinted closer at the picture. "Only difference is the mustache."

Yancy held the paper up to the light. "Ford doesn't have a mustache."

"Eugenia May does," IdaLou sniffed as she angled back to the kitchen.

That's the downside of extensive experience, which is an unsubtle euphemism for getting old. The upside is that, no matter what happens, if you're past sixty, you're acquainted with the problem and know at least three viable solutions, none of which a twenty-five-year-old wants to hear because there's no way to use a microchip or an expert on a videotape.

There are no new problems, only old problems coming around on their cycle. Unfortunately, some problems recycle so seldom that it takes a long memory to dredge up the answer. A long memory is the reason we're ratless here in Cedar Gap.

Calvin, the Born Killer

That dry spell you remember so well caused a lot of grief, not the least being that it drove a whole herd of hungry rats from the hills into town in search of water and provender.

"I've seen field mice do this in dry times," Wilson Kruddmeier said, "but never rats." He waved his thick Palace Cafe coffee mug for a refill. "That kinda infestation can drive down property values." As our district auditor, Wilson has been known to get bent all out of shape about potential tax loss.

Dodie Curnutt pointed at a grocery sack by her chair. "I've got three different kinds of rat poison in there." She squinted at one box. "But I think they mislabeled this stuff. It's really a vitamin and bran supplement for rats. They keep getting bigger and braver."

"Yeah," Newt Jimson said, "I had one big ol' buck rat out at my Gas-N-Git just flat run off my tom cat."

"You mean Tarzan backed down?" Dolly Hooter said excitedly. "I need a picture of that for next week's *Galaxy-Telegraph*."

"The way ol' Tarzan was movin', you'd better get a ticket for Milwaukee, because that's where he is right about now."

The cafe divided up into small groups telling stories of watermelon-sized rats carrying off everything up to half-grown pigs.

"You shoulda seen the one we ran out of a bar ditch yesterday," Bubba Batey yelled, startling everybody. Bubba tends toward the upper end of loud in crowds. "I thought it was a crippled dog until I saw it was a rat dragging a jack rabbit. Mean sucker!"

Yancy McWhirter stood and pounded his table for quiet. "That does it. I'm petitioning the governor and the president to declare Cedar Gap a disaster area. There's a tribe of rats under every building in town."

The hubbub of approval almost drowned out Calvin Kinchlow's muttered, "I can get rid of 'em." Calvin is the eighty-four-year-old one-eyed Linotype operator at the *Galaxy-Telegraph*.

Yancy, his state and federal grantmanship ignored, frowned at Calvin's half-bowed frizzle-haired head. "Whatta ya mean, *you* can get rid of the rats. We've tried ever'thing but dynamite and flame throwers."

Calvin's a wiry, nonsmiling five-foot-six-inch World War II veteran. But he's not just your average returning warrior. He saw action in the Pacific as a Seabee, one of those semicivilian heavy equipment operators who followed the first wave of rifles ashore to rebuild airfields and water towers. Improvisation was the name of the game on those atolls.

"Where's the worst nest?" Calvin muttered. A dozen excited voices shouted variations on "at my place," but Brenda Beth slammed down a pan and said firmly, "Right out back under our cafe storage shed."

Calvin nodded curtly. "Yancy, go over to Ambrosio's place and get me an old bicycle tube." He crippled toward the door. "The rest of you get some towsacks and shovels."

In ten minutes Calvin had his '52 Chevy panel truck backed up to the Palace Cafe's shed. He walked around the shed, bending and squinting at its foundation. Then he cut the bicycle tube, pulled one end over his Chevy's exhaust pipe and stuffed the other through a knothole in the shed's foundation.

"Awright, they ain't but one hole for 'em to come out, and that's right under the door sill. Put your sack over the hole, and when the rats run through, whack 'em with your shovel." He glowered over his old horn-rimmed glasses. "Reckon you can handle that, or did I go to fast for you?"

When he gunned the Chevy, blue smoke from depraved piston rings boiled under the shed. In seconds something bolted into the tow sack. Newt Jimson yelled and flailed at the squirming bulge.

Other shovel swingers rushed up as more and more squealing shapes fled the deadly exhaust.

In five minutes it was all over. Onlookers scattered like quail to clear their own infested houses.

The next morning Yancy called an emergency meeting of the Town Council to proclaim Calvin Kinchlow Cedar Gap's Man of the Month. Although Yancy was a bit miffed at missing still another chance to testify before a blue-ribbon panel in Washington, he did say it was a great privilege to be close friends with a genuine born killer, one who took an intuitive approach to assassination.

Calvin just frowned, pointed at his empty coffee mug, and muttered, "Sounds right to me."

Willard 'n Conrad 'n Other Warriors

For a lot of guys, war formed the high point of an otherwise pedestrian life. For few men is this more profoundly true than for Willard Ott and Conrad Dukas. Both Willard and Conrad spent the last few months of World War II making the world safe for democracy by fighting bullets, mud, and love-starved European girls.

"I 'member a little village down around Lyon," Conrad said wistfully. "We'd spent nine solid days in icy water with a forty-mile-an-hour wind. Just when I was lookin' my best, this little mademoiselle spied me, and I'll tell you, that war got a lot better fast."

"Hmmmf," Willard snorted. "Couldn't a been near as fine as those two girls that lived in that cave just outside Verona, Italy. Now, we're talkin' *grateful* when I unloaded my candy bars and Spam." He smiled broadly. "After ridin' out that landslide, those two cave girls were paradise."

Conrad frowned. "Wait a minute! I don't remember you mentionin' no landslide before."

"I didn't?" Willard pursed his lips. "Aw, *now* I remember! I called it an avalanche, like ya do if ya face death ever' day on an alp. I just made it simple for you."

"Yeah, simple! That sure describes your so-called war in Italy with all a that sunny weather. Up in France the real heroes were fightin' nose to nose with Hitler himself ever' minute. It rained eight days a week, and I know for a fact those Tiger tanks we were facin' couldn't make it across those little bitty hills in Italy to interrupt your pickin' wildflowers."

"Little hills!" Willard harumphed. "We had to drive stobs through our sleeping bags to keep from slidin' right off. You guys vacationing up in France had this nice level ground and calm rivers, nothin' like our glaciers."

"Vacation, for sure," Conrad snorted. "The Nazis in Italy had all run back home to fight us and left you to take naps in the sun and eat spaghetti." He shook his head. "We were makin' the world safe for our women while you were gettin' a suntan!"

"I cain't believe I'm sittin' here listenin' to this!" Willard unfolded another blade of his knife to whittle on a stray piece of mesquite. "We were flat worn out from beatin' Rommel in Africa before they called us to come over to fight the Mafia and Mussolini and then run up and save your hide."

"Some fight you had! One fat Italian comedian leading some Keystone Kops. Big deal! I've seen more action at our Third Thursday Dance than you had in Italy."

Willard started to answer, but Leonard Ply, the pig farmer from down near Bradshaw, wandered past. "You two still yapping about that couple of months of poor weather you called a war?" Leonard served as a gunner on a big boat in the Pacific in '44 and '45.

Willard bristled. "You hear that, Conrad? Leonard thinks eatin' coconuts and watchin' hula dancers constitutes a military offensive. Listen, that Pacific stuff was a weekend in the country compared to what me 'n Conrad had to go through."

"Nah," Leonard said placidly. "The real heroes were fighting in the Pacific back in World War II."

"Hogwash! Conrad, you 'member those troop ships we shipped over on?"

"Hard to forget. Some of those waves was higher'n the boat."

"Which made dodgin' icebergs tough."

"We both lost a lot of good friends in Europe."

"I'll tell ya one thing, I'll take our European general with two pearl-handled pistols to a full dozen of those Pacific pussywillows smokin' corncob pipes."

"Yeah!" Willard said. "It was like that time you told me about when you fell goin' after one of your shot buddies."

"Right! Or that Jeep of yours explodin'. One of us was always out gettin' shot at, and it was a lot worse'n anything Leonard ever saw."

"Boy, you got that right! Leonard never froze in French mud like you did."

"Or boiled in Africa like your outfit."

They wandered off comparing the relative merits of sailors lazing in tropical lagoons while the real warriors fought the Nazis, Communists, Mafia, weather, and grateful European women for the glory of the U.S. of A.

Yessir. Shared hardship. Talk about the tie that binds!

Ermando's Cave d'Oro

The last few days have been pretty quiet here in Cedar Gap. We've hit that doldrum period when, as Ermando Gonzales explains it, "Eet ees too late to plant and too early to pray."

Ermando is the octogenarian uncle of Ambrosio Gonzales, our intuitive mechanic. As the patriarch of the Gonzales family, Ermando feels it is his earned right and natural responsibility to show his grandchildren the inherent dignity of age while quietly watching the seasons change.

Ermando came to Texas about sixty years ago, a young Mexican from Chihuahua. He moved onto a hard-scrabble forty acres south of Cedar Gap and began plying his trade of fence mending. He did this until about 1970, when he suddenly quit working.

As he explains it, "I torn seexty years old, and my gran'sheelren needed me." He shrugs. "I save back a leetle. Concita and I do not need much, a small cornfield for tortillas, some tomato plants, a chili bush." He waves lazily toward the ancient pickup truck his nephew manages to keep running. "Eet eez not much, but eet works." A conquistador's smile moves across his face. "Thee truck an' thee driver, they are thee same. They move slow, but they move."

Ermando's financial undergirding is a constant topic in Cedar Gap conversations. "I heard once that he got some kinda pension for disarmin' a bomb back on Guadalcanal," Newt Jimson said.

"Naw," Murphy Gumpton said, "it's a pension from the Mexican government for some work he did for them right 'fore the war."

Stafford Higginbotham stirred his coffee. "I heard from a guy over in Fort Worth that Ermando was some kinda Mexican undercover agent and the Mexican police pay him to keep him quiet."

If Ermando lived anywhere but in that tiny frame house on his forty acres or if he drove a new pickup or dressed better, there might be some kind of serious inquiry. But except for his trips to San Antonio, Ermando stays pretty much to himself.

About every two months he drives to Jimson's Gas-N-Git where he catches the bus to San Antonio. When he comes back he always drops by Ornell Whapple's Feed & Lumber and the IGA Food Store for some supplies.

"'Mornin', Ermando. Need some more feed for yore ol' nanny goat?"

"Si, Meester Whapple. An' four bales of clover hay."

"Been to San Antonio again?"

"Si. To see my gran'sheelren."

"Say, Ermando, you ever fix fences any more?"

Ermando smiles. "No more. I am jus' a quiet ol' man who seets and leestens to the wind in thee cornfield and plays weeth my gran'sheelren." He pays with crisp bills, nods deferentially, and rattles away in his old '52 Dodge pickup.

Someone always bobs his head and says, "Good dude."

"Yeah, he is," someone else mutters, "but I shore do wonder where he gets his money."

"Aw, you guys haven't been talkin't to the right people. Ermando owns part of a cantina down in Nuevo Laredo that pays him a little along. I think he does right well with what he's got."

"Yeah, but I'm gettin' a little worried. Luther said he saw Ermando again last week out walkin' about two o'clock in the mornin', all bent over an' scratchin' at the foot of the mesa."

"Waaaaaal, Ol' Ermando's pushin' past eighty, so as far as I'm concerned he can do just about what he wants to do when he wants to do it. 'Sides, if it was Luther saw him, you'll have to discount about ninety percent of the sightin'."

Everybody forgot Ermando's night walks as they laughed at Luther's fabled late night liquid-fueled peregrinations and visions.

Nobody ever thinks to piece together some other information dispensed over the years, about Ermando scratching near a boulder at the foot of the mesa by the light of the moon. Or somebody seeing what looked like Ermando kneeling and digging by lantern light in his scraggly cornfield that reaches clear up to the base of the mesa. Or the fact that Bertie Faye Hogg, our postmistress, never sees a government check come through our post office for Ermando.

Nor do they tie in the small headline from a San Antonio newspaper that says, "Another Gold Doubloon from Coronado's Time Appears."

It seems that about every two months a sixteenth-century Spanish gold piece turns up in San Antonio with bits of red clay and caliche on it. Federal officers try to trace it, but they're too slow and they always lose the trail.

No one in Cedar Gap seems to know about this curious happening. Otherwise they could ask Ermando about the coin since this always happens just about the time he returns from San Antonio.

Naturally, they wouldn't interrupt his digging out near the foot of the mesa or playing with his grandchildren.

But it is a curious coincidence.

The Eight-gauge Persuasion of CoraMarie

Old dudes not only come in assorted shapes and abilities, they come in two specific genders. And, regardless of the gender, they come full of surprises, due as much as anything to their crammed-full on-board memory banks. If some trouble occurs, they don't have to search through the most recent "L.A. Law" or "thirtysomething" for some cobbled-up semianswer. They remember dirt roads and Terry and the Pirates and solving their own problems when it was 3 a.m. and they were ten miles from civilization. That gives them a whole 'nother viewpoint.

CoraMarie Minson was raking her rose garden early one morning when two stocky, square-faced men eased out of a tan pickup loaded with what appeared to be thin, white lumber.

"Nice roses, Lady."

CoraMarie, one of the most cultured and genteel women in Texas, is somewhere past seventy. She's also about four foot ten and weighs in at maybe ninety pounds. Her voice, which no one could notice above a bird's song, has never been heard in anger. Just a kind, gentle soul.

CoraMarie turned at the unknown voice. "Well, good morning, and thank you." The two leaned in toward the tiny voice.

"Nice house, too." One of the men took off his sunglasses and frowned at the upper eaves. "Hm. You got some paint peelin' there." He flicked off a piece of paint with his thumbnail. "Too bad."

Cora frowned. "Too bad about what? The paint job?"

"Naw. The dry rot." The man clambered onto the porch railing to pick at another board.

"Ah, young man, that old railing might not hold you."

"If it's as far gone as this siding, you're probably right."

CoraMarie leaned back to peer through her bifocals. "It'll look fine after the paint job next month when my check comes in."

The man shook his head sadly. "This sidin' is past helpin'." He hopped down and dusted his hands. "Tell you what. We got an introductory special on some sidin', and, . . . well, why don't we just put some on so's you can see how nice it looks. Hey, Gleeber, show this lady what her house'll look like."

"No, thank you," CoraMarie said quietly. "I'll just wait."

Gleeber began tacking strips of siding onto CoraMarie's house. The first man opened a clipboard and snapped on a form. "If you'll just sign here to show that we've put on the introductory offer, we'll . . ."

CoraMarie touched the man's arm gently. "Young man, I don't think you're listening. I don't want the sample. Now, just take it down, please."

"Lady, that siding is already on your house. Legally, you're responsible for the cost. Now, sign right . . . . Wait a minute. Where ya goin'?"

But CoraMarie, all four foot ten and ninety pounds of her, had disappeared into her house. Two minutes later they turned at her tiny voice coming from around the corner of her house.

"This pickup belong to you boys?"

"Yeah," one yelled. "Why?"

"It's got a big problem you might want to consider," she chirped.

The two aliens ran around the front porch just in time to watch CoraMarie place the butt of an enormous double-barreled shotgun against a lamppost and pull the trigger.

A deafening explosion echoed up and down Crockett Street. When the flame and smoke cleared, the right door, fender, headlight, and a sizable portion of the hood were missing from the formerly impressive pickup.

CoraMarie swung the shotgun toward the two stunned carpenters. "My granddaddy brought this eight-gauge back from Mexico about seventy years ago," she said sweetly, her smile a lovely combination of the smiles of Florence Nightingale and the Virgin Mary. "Now, please get that piece of junk off my street and out of my town." As one of the men tried to negotiate, CoraMarie sighted down the twin rain spouts cleverly disguised as gun barrels. "*Move it!*" she snarled.

They tumbled into their wounded pickup and screeched away from the curb, but not before CoraMarie braced the ancient double-barreled shotgun against a pecan tree and pulled the other trigger. The buckshot blew away the tailgate, rear fender, and spare tire.

CoraMarie Minson is back tending her roses, hobbling from bush to bush with the aid of her bent hickory cane. Those who watch closely say she stops every once in a while, moves her lips briefly, and then smiles and returns to her roses.

"You reckon those two guys frightened her into some kind of presenility?" Milo Shively said. "Kinda worries me. She never went around mumblin' like that before."

Stafford Higginbotham shook his head. "I sure hope she doesn't find out what some a the people down to the Palace Cafe have started callin' her. That'd shock her into it for sure."

Actually, those who look closely say the events may be the actual cause of the smiles. They say when CoraMarie stops, she mutters "Mad Dog Minson" a couple of times, nods approvingly, then trims another stem.

SATURDAY'S JOURNAL

AND IF I AM ELECTED . . .

ell, it's finally Saturday, the polls are closed, and Yancy is still the mayor of Cedar Gap. It's this way every two years, except this year he faced a gritty government-in-exile looking for a hostile takeover.

Yancy McWhirter, our mayor for at least twenty years, is reeling right now from the rash promises he offered to counter those promulgated by that political gadfly-in-absentia, Rudolph Pudgins.

Rudy Pudgin, you'll remember, left Cedar Gap about five years ago, but every few months he sticks his oar back in our water to suggest things like hiring the Metropolitan Opera for our civic music series and insisting that Cedar Gap is perfect for the 1992 Summer Olympics. Enraged at being ignored from afar, Rudy threatened to return, organize a palace coup, and then throw any cowardly blighters into a bar ditch who didn't agree with his platform of kamikaze progress.

"Gappies, Awake!" his posters proclaimed, the only thing lacking being his traditional "ptui" for accentuation whenever his birth city is mentioned. "Are you puke-disgusted with lackluster nondevelopment? Do you dream of Cedar Gap taking its rightful place among the great cities of the Southwest? Imagine the corporate headquarters flags of IBM and Lufthansa Airlines fluttering in the Greater Metropolitan Cedar Gap Industrial Parc! A vote for Pudgins is a vote for PROGRESS!!"

Rudy saw *parc* and *banc* and other misspellings in the *Wall Street Journal* and *TV Guide* and figured they added a nice touch to his foreign policy statements.

Yancy's eyes looked like little red-rimmed skillets as he read Rudy's posters. "He cain't get IBM and that Kraut airline in here. We haven't got enough water now! You put another five hundred people on our line, and . . ."

"More like five thousand," Leonard Ply said. "What're ya gonna do, Yancy?"

"Uh, well," Yancy stammered. "I'll have to weigh the benefits against the, uh, unbenefits." Yancy's literary invention is widely appreciated but seldom imitated.

"Hey, Yancy, Rudy says right here he can get us on the Amtrak route, only he spelled it *Amtrac*."

"Listen, y'all," Yancy pleaded, "you know as well as I do that there's no way Amtrak will come down our single spur. But I know a guy in Austin who can probably get us another daily stop on the Greyhound route to Brownwood. Ya like that idea?"

"Aw, I dunno, Yancy. Did you see that poster of Rudy's down to the Feed & Lumber saying he absolutely guaranteed us a naval training station?"

Yancy blinked at the gathering crowd, some sweat beading on his forehead. "Unless he's gonna dam up that creek on Sybil Jorgenson's back section, there's not enough water around here at one time for more than three kids with inner tubes."

"You got a better idea, Yancy?" The crowd leaned into the bloodletting. "We'd kinda like to see some sailors and big ships."

"You know, I been thinkin' about"—Yancy chewed on his lip, his eyes squinted in concentration— ". . . about, yeah, about gettin' a grant to upgrade our volunteer fire department." He glanced around. "How's that sound?"

"Weeeeell, I dunno, Yancy," Edgar Allen Plymate crooned. "Rudy's idea about scooping out the whole mesa for the world's biggest combination swimming pool and catfish ranch has an attractive ring to it."

"You any idea about how much that would . . ." Yancy skittered to a stop. "E. A., why am I wastin' time with you? You live in Winters, not here."

"Hey, now! For the chance to vote for a visionary like Mr. Pudgins, I'd seriously consider moving."

It went like that till this morning's voting. The final count was McWhirter 107, Pudgins 3.

"Yeah, I voted for Mr. Pudgins," Bubba Batey yelled. His volume goes up according to the square of the crowd size. "I'd sure like to watch them big 747s land here at our airport."

Another vote came from Luther Gravely, our area inebriate. "Rudy said he'd legalize homemade potato wine. The man's obviously a saint."

Rudy's last vote came from Sybil Jorgenson. "You bet I'd like to get Rudolph Pudgins back here, but only for about ten seconds. Just long enough so I can use a 2 × 4 on his punkin head. He wanted to grab three sections of my best stripper wells for that ridiculous industrial parc. I just want to cripple him a little."

Mostly Rudy needs to read up to see how other governments-in-exile handle their problems. Prophets in their own country, that sort of thing. It's tricky phoning in a revolution from a Seven-Eleven in Tuba City, Arizona.

CHAPTER 9

SCIENCE IN CEDAR GAP

ART OR ARTIFACT?

Wetter Isn't Always Better

ater, like cussing, is relevant to the situation. More isn't always better.

Cedar Gap has needed both more water and more pressure for years. We're at the end of a little-bitty pipe from Abilene, and as Ornell Whapple said, "I got a cow that slobbers more than my garden hose squirts."

It's common knowledge that our only answer is a water tower, but there's never been enough money in the municipal sock to pay for one. Until a month ago Tuesday.

That Tuesday, Newton Jimson, who owns the Texaco Gas-N-Git out on the highway, heard from a passing trucker about a huge water tower left stranded in San Angelo when a Wyoming company went belly up. All the hauler wanted was two hundred dollars for gas, plus a hard, flat place to unload.

The two hundred dollars we could get, but short-notice concrete is troublesome.

Newton shrugged. Yancy sighed. Ornell swore. Luther Gravely, our area inebriate, roused up on one elbow and muttered, "Rock."

Intellectually exhausted, he collapsed back on the old pew in front of the Palace Cafe.

"What'd he say?" Murphy asked.

Yancy frowned and spit. "Said 'Rock,' or somethin' like that."

"What rock?"

Luther, who was only physically paralyzed and not totally comatose, sucked in three straight shallow breaths and wheezed faintly, "Caprock."

"What'd he say 'Caprock' for?"

"'Cause it's flat and it's hard!" Ornell yelled. "Call that hauler and get 'm movin'!"

By the time the tank arrived in Cedar Gap, Bubba Batey had borrowed the highway department's road scraper and leveled a place on the edge of the mesa that looms over the east side of Cedar Gap. Two hours later the huge, silver water tank smiled down on a very thirsty little town.

"Call Carter out at the well service and see if he's got any pipe."

Carter Burkhalter allowed as how he did, in fact, have some pipe, but it was old five-inch well pipe, and he didn't think it was exactly . . .

"Don't make excuses, Carter! Get a load of it here and hook us up. We got us a water tower!"

Carter never wants to make a fuss, even when eyeballing a guaranteed disaster. First, he hitched up the little pipe from the Abilene Water Company so the tank could start filling. He worked straight through, until along about sundown Thursday when he waved his hat to say he'd welded the last section of pipe in place. A shout went up that could have been heard in Tijuana because everybody just knew, "We got water pressure at last!"

Well, yes and no. Mayor Yancy bounced his old International Scout up the mesa to the main valve, unfurled a Texas flag, and then yanked the valve handle.

A solid five-inch torpedo of water dropped almost straight down through the rusty pipe. As it headed across the slope of the mesa it built speed and noise until it funneled into the main Cedar Gap lines with the snarling power of a mountain freight.

When the squeezed water arrived downtown, all four city fire hydrants erupted in sequence like valve lifters on a Farmall tractor. The water tap in Corinne Iverson's Fountainebleau Beauty Spa hair-washing sink blew off. Then the greasy, rusty water bent around the little basin and blasted off through the dropped ceiling of accoustic tile like a deer rifle bullet shot through Kleenex.

All over town the filthy water knocked faucets off sinks and split garden hoses their entire lengths. It was fortunate nobody was using the toilet in the post office because the porcelain facility blew completely through the wall and out into the street.

Mayor Yancy, still up on the mesa, took the roar of the water and the screaming of the populace as his rightful homage. He stuck his Texas flag in the Scout wheel well and drove majestically downhill toward his expected triumphal entry only to dodge Bubba Batey careening around a corner in the highway department's road scraper screaming, "Where's the water pipe?"

Bubba dropped the blade, caught it on Carter's rusty pipeline, and backed up until it snapped. The water pipe flopped around like a runover snake until it ran dry.

But you can't count the week a total loss.

Early that Friday morning Carter managed to rejoin the original line, so we're at least back to where we were.

Bubba was considered a kind of minor-league savior, a confusing mindset we're still working on.

That night the Cedar Gap Independent Full Gospel Non-Denominational Four Square Missionarian Church of the Apostolic Believers sponsored a special prayer service and potluck supper of thanks for the water that does make it through.

It all works out. It's all relevant.

If "Save the Whales" Won't Fly, Then . . .

Well, it's finally quieted down here in Cedar Gap. There for a while we were just on the brim of getting organized, a terrifying thought.

The problem started with our bimonthly-or-so letter from Rudolph Pudgins. Rudy, you'll remember, is our expert expatriot who currently lives as a voluntary high dudgeon exile in Tuba City, Arizona. Every so often his West Texas genetic substructure short-circuits, forcing him to cadge some stationery from the Motel 6 and give us the double-barreled benefits of his desert solitude. For pure value of invention, his letters rank right up there with pet rocks and the Nehru jacket.

Dolly Hooter, the official reader of Pudginian grandiloquence, rolled her eyes heavenward when Bertie Faye Hogg ceremoniously dropped the small package from Rudy on the Palace Cafe counter. As our Cedar Gap postmistress, Bertie Faye feels a hand-delivered letter "adds that little personal touch to an otherwise bureaucratic quagmire."

Dolly picked up the oversized letter. "Why," she asked slowly, "do I always get this feeling of impending doom every time I see Rudy's scribbled name on an envelope?"

Corley Freemont squinted out the window. "Prob'ly 'cause ever' time Rudy writes, our whole world goes about two degrees off plumb. What's he up to this time?"

The local consensus is that Rudy's letters are a whole lot like a train wreck: they're spectacular while they're in progress, and although they tend to clutter up the landscape, the debris is always fascinating. The Palace Cafe crowd leaned back, rabbity apprehension and ghoulish curiosity mixed in about equal parts.

"Hmm," Dolly mumbled. "That's funny. There's a little envelope wrapped inside the main letter." She squinted at the scrawled writing. "It says to read the letter first."

Rudy's letter:

"Dear Gappies: Ptui! [Expectorant punctuation is a given in Rudy's missives whenever his natal city is mentioned.] Oh, yes, I remember very well how you rejected me for mayor—another skunk-puke example of Cedar Gap's (ptui) blind aversion to progress. Still, my strength is as the strength of ten because my heart is pure. And your miserable blindness demands my concern and therefore this letter.

"ARISE AND AWAKE, YE BLIND!

"Bit by ghastly bit our Texas wildlife is being destroyed by unfettered progress. Things are dying! First, the saber-toothed tiger, then the carrier pigeons. Now . . . THIS!! And in Cedar Gap! Paaaaahtui!"

Stafford Higginbotham shook his head as if to clear it. "T. Edsel's

Thanksgivin' sermon comparin' Original Sin to a dull chain saw was clearer than that letter. What's he talkin' about, anybody got any idea?"

Dolly flapped Rudy's letter in the air. "Let me finish."

Rudy's second page: "Sure, you say, we've still got buzzards and deer ticks. But if Brontosaurus Rex is gone, can mankind be far behind?

"Join our parade! Save our Texas heritage! Work those Cedar Gap (ptui) committees you've been assigned."

Bewildered glances filled the cafe. "What committees?" Vera Frudenburg asked. "The only committee Rudolph Pudgins was ever on decorated our elementary school Christmas tree with snuff cans and beer pulls."

"Now, wait a minute, Vera," Murphy Gumpton said, "that was a great tree. I remember . . ."

"Hush, Murph," Dolly said. "There's only one more sentence to the letter." Silence fell like a curtain. "Rudy says, 'Open the envelope.' "

The Palace Cafe's anxiety meter pegged upward as Dolly ripped open the second envelope. She lifted out a long piece of paper folded in zigzag fashion, snorted as she read it, and then walked to the bulletin board by the cash register to thumbtack the banner for everyone to read.

The cafe erupted as half the people yelled in anger and the other half fell over laughing. The banner, a multicolor melange of Crayolas on butcher paper, read:

> SAVE THE FIRE ANTS!
> NATIONAL HEADQUARTERS!
> YOU COULD BE NEXT!!

There's your problem with Rudy Pudgins: he sneaks just enough truth in his fatuous pronouncements to confuse an otherwise relaxed citizenry.

Leonard Ply leaned back in his creaky chair. "You know, the best thing we did this year was keep Rudy out of the mayor's office."

"I dunno, Leonard," Milo Shively said. "That kind of invention should be utilized somehow. As I think about it, he'd probably make a pretty good king."

Brenda Beth Kollwood paused in mid-refill, her coffee pot hovering. "That's got a nice ring to it." She tilted her head as she mulled it over. "King Rudolph of Cedar Gap."

Fourteen people said, "Ptui!"

All Visitors Are Welcome in Our Town

Science in Cedar Gap stays pretty well in the category of pragmatic application. We know what makes plants grow and what makes pickups stall. If academic investigation gets much beyond that, there's a tendency to leave it for the science teachers down at the high school. We're still trying to figure out that night when Donnie Sue Kingsbury almost tracked down . . . something.

Donnie Sue, you'll remember, is our diminutive deputy sheriff assigned to this part of the county. She's a wonderful girl despite her border patrol nickname of "Chain Saw" and her penchant for pulling her .44 magnum to solve otherwise smallish problems.

On that Tuesday evening Donnie Sue kept to her weekly habit of slowly driving up the gravel road a mile or so south of Cedar Gap. "Ya never know," she said. "Found a bootlegger there once." Bootlegging was the only thing on her mind when she spotted two small red lights blinking out of a thicket on the top edge of the mesa.

"I eased over and cut the engine." Donnie Sue frowned at the memory, and then slowly stirred her Palace Cafe coffee. "I figured it might be hunters, but it was more likely somebody runnin' a still. Then I noticed the red lights didn't bob up and down like they were being carried." She slurped the steaming coffee. "Those red dots just sorta glided along, real smooth, like they were on a wire."

Everybody in the cafe leaned forward. They'd heard the bare-bones story several times, but new elements kept surfacing.

She grimaced. "I edged into a cedar break, figurin' I'd . . ."

"Were you follerin' the lights?" somebody asked.

Donnie Sue nodded carefully. "Sorta. But they were movin' awful fast, jerkin' back and forth, and sometimes they disappeared completely."

As she crept through the thick cedar stalking the red lights, she missed seeing two bent forms stumbling down the steep, rocky side of the mesa off to her right. Suddenly a tremendous thrashing and swearing exploded out of a patch of shinnery. Rattling rocks and gargled vilification mixed in the dim light as Donnie Sue clawed at her .44 and yelled, "Get outa there or you're dog meat!"

A two-second silence was followed by piercing screams as the leaping forms clawed their way back up the loose shale of the mesa.

Donnie Sue aimed her .44 at a rock outcropping near the brow of the mesa. Three thundering shots brought a huge slab of limestone crashing end over end down the steep hillside. The two scrambling figures squalled again as they lurched into a bramble-filled gulch out of the way of the tumbling rock.

"Hands in the air," Donnie Sue shouted, "or I'll collect you like a bucket a rotten tomatoes." As she waved the cannonlike revolver at the now-quiet shinnery, from the corner of her eye she saw the two red globes pop up over the edge of the mesa several yards apart.

"Awright, you two up on the hill, get down here!"

Abruptly the two lights zipped together, as she explained, "like a cross-eyed cat in the dark." Startled, Donnie Sue swung her .44 at the lights, but they pulled back into a thicket and disappeared.

"I'll get you two up there on the hill in a minute, as soon as I . . . Luther! What in the ever-lovin' . . . . *Bubba*? Is that you?" She stalked toward the quailing men.

The two stumbled toward her, blubbering and yelling not to shoot. "We was just pickin' up some wild pecans," Bubba stuttered. "We thought you was one of those two dopeheads up on the mesa."

Donnie Sue squinted at the two scratched and tattered misfits. "Two what's?"

Luther Gravely, his shirt ripped and blood dripping from a cut chin, pointed toward the mesa. "We stumbled on a couple a guys up there in that big cedar brake just beyond the brow of the hill. We figured they must be using the mesa for some freelance snorting because they were wearing those silver uniforms like firefighters wear."

"Yeah," Bubba said, "with a silver helmet and gloves, except they had some kinda cigar or flashlight or somethin' in their helmets that made their facemasks glow real bright red."

That was when Donnie Sue decided to check out the mesa at sunup.

"What'd ya find, Donnie Sue?" somebody asked excitedly.

The short, stocky deputy sheriff stared into her coffee a long time and then let her eyes focus past the window onto the distant hillside. "Three burnt places like campfires, only they were in a perfect triangle." She hesitated. "But no ashes, only blackened rock, like three big blowtorches had been there." Her fingers tapped nervously on the mug handle. "And a funny musky smell." Then she walked out.

Everyone leaned back, afraid to speak. Presently they all got up quietly and left. Some things are best left undiscussed, even in Cedar Gap.

SATURDAY'S JOURNAL

LUTHER THE MIDPERSON

ell, it's Saturday again here in Cedar Gap, and Luther is nowhere to be found. That generally means he's in the middle of an important four-bottle session of R&R in a hunting cabin up on the mesa. We usually don't defend Luther's bacchanalian tendencies, but given last Thursday morning, we understand.

Luther "20–20" Gravely, has built a career trying to remember what it was he was drinking to forget. He thinks it had something to do with Cambodia and an herbal proctologist, but he's a bit hazy on particulars.

Thursday morning was actually the end of Wednesday night for Luther. He'd finished a batch of homemade potato wine and was determined that it wouldn't age too thoroughly. "Catch it past its peak and you lose the poetry."

"What's it's optimum age, Luther?"

"About six minutes. After that, it tends to rust."

Luther had rustproofed about a gallon of Gravely's Ol' Frog Sweat, his personal designer hooch, by the time he wandered down off the mesa. He walked carefully, protecting a headache that, if it were an earthquake, would measure 8.7 and devastate India. Then he saw the car. And the young woman. The extraordinarily bulbous and noisy young woman.

"Aah! Aaah! *Aaaaaarrrrgh*!!" she yelled. Luther recoiled from the excruciating noise. She spied him. "Sir! *Sir*! Can you—*Aaaarrrgh*!—help me? Please?"

"I'll help, but you can't yell. Is your car out of gas, or what?"

"No, I'm—*Eeeaagh*!—going to have a baby."

"Look, I know you're happy, but please, *please*, don't scream!"

"*No*!" she gasped, "I'm going to—*Aaargggh*!—have my babies right now!"

An arctic chill blew through Luther. "We gotta get you to . . ."

"No—*Wrrrrrooowr*!—time. You've got to help me."

Brief flashes of Butterfly McQueen squinching out "I ain't never birthed no babies" tiptoed through the tiny fragment of Luther's brain that was still operative. He sank carefully onto a large boulder, only to be kicked vertical by another gorilla yell.

"It's coming! *It's coming*!"

Luther's mouth tasted like the inside of a three-day dead carp, and his vital signs were dropping toward zero. But somewhere down his brain stem he dredged up a rerun of an old television special on rhinocerous birthings on the African veldt.

"I suppose it'd be too much to ask you to get up on your knees and munch some weeds." Luther barely got his fingers in his ears before another simian screech erupted from the woman's shaking head.

Slowly, with no conscious control of his actions, Luther Gravely followed the script of that "Wild Kingdom" show. The potential mother's staccato prayers for deliverance mixing with profane vilification of her absent husband were easily the equal of the enraged rhino's bellowing roar.

But Luther heard nothing. His pickled mind abruptly realized that if one more sound penetrated a brain cell his entire head would explode. At that instant of self-knowledge, Luther's world turned into a cotton ball. Serenely, he watched his arms move like wisps of vapor, without sensation or effort, in tomblike silence.

Within three minutes he lifted an untidy, wrinkled football-like object and laid it on the woman's chest. Another three minutes and the young mother had a matched set of footballs. Luther sat back to admire the sports equipment while the woman, covered with sweat and slick babies, gasped a faint "Thank you."

The first car Luther flagged down contained Deputy Sheriff Donnie Sue Kingsbury coming off a graveyard shift. They eased the mother and twins into the squad car, but Luther decided it was such a lovely, quiet morning he'd much rather walk to town.

An hour later he sat slumped over a steaming cup of coffee at the Palace Cafe counter. Donnie Sue, grinning widely, slammed through the door.

"'Mornin', Sheriff," Luther said placidly. "Up kinda early, aren't you?"

Donnie Sue's grin faded. She peered at Luther's hunched form. "I thought you might like to know that the mother and twins are fine."

Luther turned on the squeaky stool. "What mother?"

She looked around at a roomful of puzzled faces. "Didn't you tell 'em?"

Luther slurped his coffee, then said mildly, "Tell 'em what? What're you talkin' about?"

It seems Luther remembered not a single moment of his skyrocket medical career.

Stafford Higginbotham attempted to clarify the problem. "When you vacation on Mars like Luther, you tend to lose information during the reentry burn."

That would probably explain a lot of things.

It won't explain Luther, but it would probably explain a lot of things.

CHAPTER 10

ACTUALLY, THEY'RE KINDA

HARD TO DESCRIBE

Well, He Ain't Ol' Doc Winslow!

For as long as anybody can remember, Elmer Winslow has been called Ol' Doc Winslow. Feeling his years, Doc found a shiny new family practice physician from down around Corpus named Dr. Danny Plunkett. Unfortunately, Danny's thirty, looks eighteen and sounds twelve. His greatest problem, as delineated by Dodie Curnutt, is he's "cute."

"That mean he's your new doctor?" Murphy Gumpton asked.

"Murphy, are you totally outa your mind? Listen, there's places on me even *I* haven't seen, and no kid who looks younger'n my daughter is going to check my references."

Arnold, Dodie's husband, nodded and frowned. "The mechanic oughta be at least as old as the car."

"Well, Ol' Doc Winslow recommended him."

"You seen him? I swear I heard his voice break, and he didn't even have socks on."

It went downhill from there. The prognosis for Dr. Danny's survival, much less his success, looked bleak. Or it was until he'd been here about a month. Danny sat hunched over some pancakes here in the Palace Cafe when Roo Blint walked in slowly, his face scrunched with pain.

"Gimme some coffee," Roo commanded.

Brenda Beth Kollwood, our best waitress, figured Roo was just hungry. "How about some breakfast to go with it?"

"When I want breakfast I'll ask for it," Roo snarled. He turned and staggered toward a chair, the coffee sloshing onto the floor.

Ruben Blint lives a few miles south of town on a useless half section. It wasn't always useless. Roo just let the soil and fences go until even the weeds were sorry and stunted, and there was no way to pen up his cattle. Nancy, his wife, had to go to work, his kids left the minute they turned sixteen, and Roo took up drinking as a vocation. Most folks think he was a wife beater, but nobody could prove anything and Nancy never let on.

Across the Palace Cafe, Danny stopped eating. He watched closely as Roo massaged his left arm, then hunched his shoulder like he'd eaten too many jalapeños on his chili.

Danny walked over to Roo. "Uh, sir, are you having some problems?"

Roo glanced sideways at Danny. "Get outa here, kid."

"I'm a doctor, and I don't like the way you're rubbing that arm. Do you have a history of heart trouble?"

Roo swore under his breath. "You're no doctor, you're a snot-nosed kid. Leave me alone. I've just got a little gas."

"Gas won't make your arm ache, but a coronary will. You'd better lie down while we call an ambulance."

"No pimply-faced baby's gonna tell me what to do!" Roo lurched to his feet and threw his coffee on Danny's shirt.

Danny never changed his expression. "Miss Kollwood, call for an ambulance. Sir, calm down or you could bring on a heart attack. Why don't you just . . ."

Roo flung his heavy coffee cup against the wall, shattering a picture. "You and my wife, both tryin' to tell me how to act." He lunged toward Danny. "I'll do the same to you as I did to her, except you'll be more . . ." Suddenly, Roo's face twisted in a silent scream as he collapsed full length on the floor, his fists still clenched.

Danny worked fast, trying every life-saving technique he knew. But Ruben Blint was dead, done in by liquor and pure malignant meanness.

After the ambulance left, the Palace Cafe crowd swarmed around Dr. Danny Plunkett, complimenting him on his resuscitative efforts.

"I'm puttin' Danny up for Citizen of the Month," Yancy Mc-Whirter said later. "The way I figure it he's kind of a hero, seein' as how he took care of one of our nastier problems. I just can't think what we oughta call him."

"We cain t call him Doc," Leonard Ply said. "Elmer's already got that name nailed."

"Someday," Dodie Curnutt said, "when Elmer's gone, we can call Danny Doc. But we need something else right now. How about Little Doc?"

Arnold Curnutt grinned. "How about Dr. Death?"

Everybody smiled and nodded. But Brenda Beth said sternly, "Now, you be nice to Danny. He might save your life sometime."

Of course, Little Doc is Danny's name out in public. But in private meetings the story of Roo's sudden demise will be polished and augmented, and the name of Dr. Death will surface. Oh, yes, it definitely will.

It's a good name. As Arnold said, "We'd only use that kind a name on somebody we liked."

And that's the truth. But it'll flat scare you to think of them *not* liking him.

Our Man in Moscow

A couple of months ago Yancy McWhirter, our dollar-a-year mayor of two decades, noticed an article in a professional journal saying mayors from modest-sized metropolises could apply for a special ten-day City Leader's Tour of Russia. Yancy twirled his coffee at the same time that he twirled the idea of an expense-paid fact-finding trip to the motherland of Communism. He never figured on actually getting the trip, so when he got the news he'd been accepted, Yancy's coffee hand trembled more than a bit as he said, "I've been to Fort Worth and Denver, but I understand Moscow's a little different."

Since the glasnost-addled Intourist Travel Agency handled all arrangements, they insisted that the group of twelve small-town mayors fly Aeroflot, Russia's national airline.

"That airline could flat use some decoratin' help. You know that green scum that forms on the drainage ditch out behind our fire department? That's the main decorative color for Aeroflot planes. The walls and seat covers all look like a runover frog."

"How was the food, Yancy?"

Our mayor, who considers four-alarm chili as mother's milk and claims he used a jalapeño pepper for his pacifier, blanched at the memory. "I'll have to stay with generalities because there are ladies present. The main problem was, nothin' looked like anything I'd ever eaten before. They had a little paper cup of somethin' that looked like a handful of goat heads in two-week-old brown Jello."

"What'd they call it, Yancy?"

"Dessert."

Combining the pig-knuckle pudding with ten hours of jet lag made Yancy's face a perfect color match for the Aeroflot seat covers when he deplaned at the Moscow airport. But his main problems came with his trip to the country.

"They put us on this overnight train that Lenin must have used in World War I. I've fallen down hills that were more comfortable. Then the farm equipment they kept braggin' about, what there was of it, was seriously outdated. And ugly! Now, I'm not sayin' a plow's got to be designed by Rembrandt or Mozart, but it should look like it was at least built in this century! Ever' tractor I saw looked forever like that cotton planter that Ambrosio pieced together."

Ambrosio Gonzales, Cedar Gap's intuitive mechanic, is famed in story and song for his improvised vehicles. Yancy was referring to a four-row cotton planter Ambrosio crafted out of a '37 Packard frame, a crashed Piper Cub, and an eight-sucker milking machine.

"Were the people as mean as we've heard, Yancy?" somebody asked.

Yancy hesitated. He got a faraway look in his eyes as his voice gentled. "You know, I met a Russian mayor over there who ran a little town just about the size of Cedar Gap. Of course, his town didn't have paved streets or a fire department, and their one little bitty street light had about a 25-watt bulb in it. But, ya know, the rest of his problems are exactly what I run into."

"Now, come on, Yancy, you got no problems here in the Gap!"

Yancy frowned over his glasses at the heckler. "That mayor, Sergei Something-or-other, said he had wonderful people in his town who just keep tryin' to get through another year without goin' broke. And even when the weather is against them, which is about ever' year according to Sergei's reckoning, the rest of the people in town always help out whoever is the worst off."

The listeners looked at each other and nodded knowingly. "You mean, they got trouble with dust storms and no rain in Russia?"

"Try snow storms and no roads," Yancy said softly. "Sergei's tried for years to get a truck with snow tires so they can get sick kids and injured adults to the nearest doctor, who's about fifty miles away over roads that are worse than the roads we've abandoned in this county. But Sergei just smiled and said he'd keep tryin', because that's what mayors do."

"Well, we're glad you made it home, Yancy."

Our mayor nodded as he looked out the Palace Cafe window. "All I could think of on the flight back from Moscow was Sergei and his little town and how he loved those terrible streets and the miserable winter weather. But most of all he just flat loved the people who lived there." He hesistated. "Sorta like . . ."

Yancy turned away from the crowd and blew his nose.

"He must have caught a little cold on the trip home," Brenda Beth said. All those listening nodded understandingly and looked back at their coffee.

Knotholes Are Us

Well, it's been a profitable few days here in Cedar Gap. Although both General Motors and DeBeer's Diamond Mines refused our offer of land so they could move their corporate headquarters here—that was Rudy Pudgins' concept for his Greater Metropolitan Cedar Gap Industrial Parc—we still have a higher than normal level of raw entrepreneurial spirit. Just the same, success can be debilitating.

Back last spring, Sparky Coyle, our free-lance carpenter, was picking up his scraps after installing some cabinets for Sybil Jorgenson when Sybil's grandniece wandered in. "Now, Becky Lynn, watch out for those saws," Sparky told the kindergartner. "They're sharp. Here, play with these scraps. They're not worth anything."

The little girl's eyes widened at the odd shaped and fragrant pieces of pine. She stuffed every splinter and chip she could find in an old canvas bag, and then toted them out on Sybil's wide veranda.

That night Sparky's phone rang. "Sparky, this is Sybil. Listen, you got any more of those scraps like you gave Becky Lynn?"

"I dunno. There may be a few out back sommers. Why?"

"Becky Lynn's got three of her friends staying the night, and they're fighting because there aren't enough knotholes to go around."

"Hmm. Lemme see. I could scrape up a few, I suppose. What'sa matter with the rest of their toys?"

"Nothing, except nobody'll play with anything but those knotty wood scraps you gave Becky Lynn."

"Kids!" he snorted. "OK, I'll find ya some knots."

The next day Becky Lynn took the blocks to school for Show and Tell. That afternoon Sparky got five calls from frustrated parents wanting to know where they could buy some blocks "just like the ones Becky Lynn brought to school."

"Look," he said, "they ain't nothin' but scrap wood. G'wan down to Whapple's Feed & Lumber and get some 1 × 2s and cut your own."

But that wouldn't work for the parents of snuffling kids, so Sparky spent the whole evening cutting up old 2 × 4s and reclaimed planks. Unfortunately, Sparky missed the critical element in the wood—knots.

The kids spent about twelve seconds with the blocks.

"These aren't as neat as Becky Lynn's."

"Now, look, Mr. Coyle made those blocks special just for you."

"But there aren't any funny shapes on them."

Dial-dial-dial. "Hello, Sparky? We got us a little problem."

Sparky threw up his hands in frustration. Since he prided himself on the quality of his wood, he could only shrug as he pawed through his stack of odd-sized lumber for knotholes. Then he spied the rack of mesquite firewood drying next to his garage. An hour later he called the five parents. "You want knotholes? I got knotholes. Come 'n get 'em."

That solved Sparky's problem until a kid from Dallas visiting his Cedar Gap cousin carried a few of the blocks back home to the big city.

Dial-dial-dial. "Hello, Mr. Coyle? This is Humbert Williams at the Dallas Toy Mart. I'd like to talk to you about the possibility of your firm making, oh, say, a thousand units of those free-form educational block sets my grandson brought back from Cedar Gap."

Sparky went looking for knotholes. He found a pile of discarded cedar fence posts. Then he tore down the old privy behind the volunteer fire department. Finally he cut half an acre of stunted mesquite. Sparky pulled his overhead saw back and forth until his arm cramped. The pile of knotholes grew.

About an hour ago Sparky got back from delivering the last of the thousand sacks of wood scraps to the Dallas toy man.

"Hey, Sparky, what'd that lady from the Dallas newspaper want when she phoned?"

"Aw, that weren't nothin'. She just called to ask how I came up with my theory of makin' toys that don't look like toys."

"What'dja tell her?"

"I told her I just figured the more a toy looks like somethin' real, the less a kid can do with it. If it only looks like a piece a wood, then you can call it what you want. A knothole can be a target or a stove lid or might near anything." Sparky shrugged and stirred his coffee. "I don't think she bought into that theory just a whole bunch."

"You got any more orders, Sparky?" somebody yelled from across the Palace Cafe.

"I dunno," Sparky said wearily. "I kinda hope not."

"What's a matter, don't you like makin' money?"

"It ain't that." He stared into his coffee cup. "It's just that cuttin' off the good wood an' throwin' it away an' only keepin' the knotholes finally got to me. I got so nervous I couldn't sleep nights."

Integrity will do funny things to you.

SATURDAY'S JOURNAL

THE SANCTIFIED MESSAGE OF

BROTHER WOODY

ell, it's Saturday here in Cedar Gap, and it's a lot quieter than yesterday evening. Woody's on the bus, headed east.

The problem started three days ago when Woodard Hafferhan, a thirty-two-year-old part-time jackleg carpenter, had an out-of-body experience that was almost an out-of-this-world experience. His car got hit by our only train, the once-a-month Sante Fe freight, that left him sitting on a smouldering seat cushion watching the rest of his '74 Impala explode in a gully.

What saved him was his relaxed attitude, the product of two quarts of Thunderbird and a six-pack of Mexican beer. When the image of the flame-scarred wreckage finally seeped into his alcohol-marinated brain, two things happened: Woody fainted in a heap. Then when he roused, he got a vision that out-glowed St. Paul's.

"Hallelujah, I'm answering your CALL!" Woody screamed, startling the volunteer fire department crew that answered the fire alarm. "Yo! I'm right here, and the answer is YES! JUST GIMME A MESSAGE!"

Broadus Trilby and Norman Underwood lowered their fire hose

and glanced uneasily at each other and then at Woody. "Uh, Woody, you didn't by any chance bang your head when you tumbled out of your car, did you?"

But all Woody could do was screech like a dispeptic panther and wave his hands at the clouds. Obviously, he was hearing suggestions from somewhere else and wanted whoever was talking to know that he was definitely willing to take requests.

That was Wednesday. All day Thursday he wandered the streets as a free-lance tub-thumping missionary, buttonholing startled citizens and generally being misinterpreted. By Friday he realized that, if Woodard Hafferhan was to mutate into Brother Woodard Hafferhan, the Bearer of the Message, it was obvious he would need a base of operations. He vaguely remembered that, as a teenager, he had a fleeting but memorable relationship with a deacon's daughter in the little congregation of the Church of the Apostolic Believers that met down in Brownwood. He mulled the memory over. Close enough. He stumbled to the Cedar Gap Apostolic Believers parsonage door and knocked.

"BROTHER PEDIGREW, I'M BROTHER WOODY, AND I'M HERE!" Woody shouted, his lips six inches from the recoiling ears of T. Edsel Pedigrew, the portly pastor of the Cedar Gap Independent Full-Gospel Non-Denominational Four-Square Missionarian Church of the Apostolic Believers. "I've been sent for, and you gotta believe that I AM READY!"

T. Edsel blinked against the high-decibel screeching. "Ahhhhh, yes, Wood. . . , ah, *Brother* Woody. Ummmm, . . . could you share with me just exactly *what* it is you are ready for?"

"SAVIN' ALL THOSE LOST WRETCHES ADDICTED TO WHATEVER!" Woody yelled. Then, in a whisper, "I must preach to every poor, benighted"—who knows where he came up with that word—"soul lost in alcoholic and other profound error." An exploding car and a rap on the head released hitherto untapped fountains of Hafferhan verbiage.

T. Edsel yo-yoed forth and back with the yelling and the whispering. "Uhhh, . . . well, Brother Woody," he glanced around. "There doesn't seem to be too many of them on the streets tonight, so maybe you could . . ."

Woody straightened and glared at a light that came on in the Apostolic Believers' big classroom. "Somebody's in there," he said darkly.

"That's just Sister Oliphant and our Sanctuary Committee ladies starting their weekly . . ."

"I'LL SAVE 'EM!" Woody shouted as he careened through the sanctuary searching for salvageable humanoids. Sister Oliphant, a statuesque pouter pigeon with a perpetual glare of stern disapproval, turned at the galumphing Hafferhan brogans. She was greeted with "REPENT, YOU TOAD-SUCKIN' SINNER!"

T. Edsel cringed at the expected explosion. Instead, a benevolent smile spread under the arched brows and glacial eyes of the Keeper of the Apostolic Flame.

"And you are. . . ?" she asked smoothly.

"BROTHER WOODY!"

"And what, Brother Woody, do you wish to do with your life?"

"SAVE EVERY GRAVY-SWILLIN', BACKSLIDIN' REPROBATE I CAN GET MY HANDS ON!"

Sister Oliphant lowered her voice conspiratorily. "And where, Brother Woody, would you find large groups of these sorts of people?"

Three straight questions for Woody's fogged mind pushed probability, but finally his head shook, his lips pursed, and he yelled, "MOSCOW!"

For the next hour T. Edsel stood transfixed as Sister Oliphant coached Woodard Hafferhan on the proper stance and vocal inflection for his one-man march in front of the Soviet embassy in Washington, D.C. She even painted "Let Me IN!" on a nursery sheet that could be used as a banner, a nice touch certain to be appreciated by the embassy guards. She also paid half of Woody's one-way bus ticket to Washington.

So, Woody's on his missionary journey. He should make it in about three days. If the bus driver doesn't convert first. Or defect.

CHAPTER 11

THE FINEST TOWN

ANYWHERES AROUND HERE

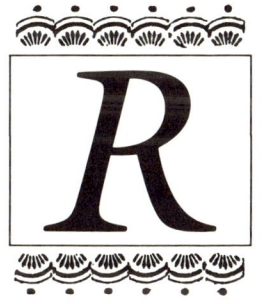

Yes, Sir, It's the Finest

Recently a whole passel of citizens sat around the Palace Cafe reading copies of a little brochure that had just arrived in the mail. Some state agency printed up a two-color 3 × 8 giveaway, *Visit Beautiful Cedar Gap*, for visitor centers around Texas.

"I figured that, given our extensive history, it'd be twelve, fifteen pages at least," Yancy McWhirter said. "It looks like they just took a piece a typin' paper and folded it twice. I'd call that sorry work."

Brenda Beth Kollwood sensed the surge of a surly mob and began splashing coffee in half-full mugs. "It looks as if they ran out of information."

"Yeah," Milo Shivley muttered. "The whole thing sounds like a bunch of generic paragraphs left over from some Farm Bureau bulletin." He glanced around. "We could write our own and do better'n this."

A hubbub of "You bet" and "That's for sure" boiled out of the tight-lipped group.

"Well, what's stoppin' us?" Milo shouted. "Brenda Beth, dig out that stack of year-old menus you keep under the counter. We'll write on those. Listen up, y'all. I want a good solid paragraph about somethin' that's important to Cedar Gap."

Of such virulent fervor is revolution born. That call to action formed the genesis of the *Authentic Cedar Gap History and Artifact Booklet*, which ballooned to 210 pages with leatherette cover and plastic comb binding. Chapters ran from *Automotive* (a listing of prewar vehicles still bouncing around the county) to *Xeriscape* (waterless landscaping in which spiny weeds are considered beautiful) in a literary style ranging from late Victorian gush to improvisational anger. While the phrasing often resembled the bawling of a brain-damaged steer, the one constant was passion.

"Ah, the achingly beautiful sea-green tendrils of our newly sprung April mesquite," Sybil Jorgenson wrote in her tribute to the tree that will grow anywhere. "Almost frail in its laciness but sturdy as a lug wrench, our omnipresent harbinger of the vernal season flaunts the glory of robust Nature."

Sybil's girlhood was spent reading tragic turn-of-the-century novels by lady authors with three names and a penchant for adjectival overload.

On the opposite end of the literary plank stands Jakub Mielczewski, a Polish transplant, whose vernacular mixes Krakovian freedom-fighter rhetoric with a Texas newcomer's euphoria. "Clear-eyed warriors settled Gap, men with joy of freedom and happiness of sweat. Polish blood part of land now. Not beautiful like sunrise over Krakow, but sunrise over mesa still unbelievable." Strategic words, such as articles, tend to get lost in Jakub's grandiloquent style, but the sinewy vigor comes through clearly.

Of course, Dolly Hooter, the *Cedar Gap Galaxy-Telegraph*'s most inventive reporter, produced one of her legendary punkin-vine sentences honoring a World War I hero.

"Corporal D. T. 'Shoat' Trilby, whose nickname appeared after a neighbor's prize shoat, a three-month-old Poland China of purebred lineage, allegedly disappeared into some of Shoat's sausage casings in 1922, but was later proven to have been borrowed for breeding purposes but whose papers—the shoat's papers, not Shoat's papers—never appeared, fired while hunting a wild pig, which Shoat averred was much like a Poland China only from Germany or France, he'd forgotten which, and accidently blew up an ammunition dump, which was German, but the pig, which didn't survive the explosion, wasn't."

Bubba Batey's literary rope has a slipknot on both ends. He produced an impassioned defense of roadside mowers. "Mowing is important. I am a mower. If it wasn't for us you'd be up to your [several words were scratched out on the original brown paper sack manuscript] up to your *whatever* in Johnson grass and goatheads. We are important. Anybody says we ain't better take it back or get licked."

The opening descriptive material of the *History and Artifact Booklet* contained the finest bits of Utopian invention.

The mesa hovering east of Cedar Gap became the "towering menace of limestone and cedar glowering down on a noble village."

The area's red clay was said to grow "prodigious crops to nourish vital men and women in the tradition of Crockett, Bowie, and the Vikings."

"Vast vistas of azure sky and rich turf call to the wanderer that here is luxury, here is provender, here is home."

And that was only the first paragraph. After that it got sort of flowery. Dolly's Instamatic illustrations managed to get every building in town behind the single oak tree on Main Street.

As Corley Freemont said, "That brochure makes me want to move to Dallas just so's I could vacation back here."

Well, what's a travel brochure for?

The Fourth Estate, Cedar Gap Style

Our regular Friday edition of the *Cedar Gap Galaxy-Telegraph* always comes off the giant press early Saturday morning. The fact that it's always Saturday when the paper appears bothers the citizenry not a whit. As Dolly Hooter, our ace reporter, continually reminds us, "News is like pizza. If it won't last twenty-four hours it was sorry to begin with."

Since the eight pages of our *Galaxy-Telegraph* has to cover all news from Main Streetian to intergalactic, the editorial details tend to be skimpy and the mix curious. Every Saturday this prompts muttered asides that give the Palace Cafe the verbal texture of morning practice in a monastery.

"This is the third straight week we've had a recipe for barbecued possum," Waldo Beeler said. "I'll donate five dollars to anybody who'll burn that Cajun cookbook Dolly bought in New Orleans."

"That's not your main problem," Corley Freemont said, shaking his head. "Does Dolly actually believe anybody in either Texas or their right mind truly cares who won a hockey game in Edmonton?"

Oliver Greenslope snapped his paper and then snorted. "I see the *Galaxy-Telegraph*'s keepin' up its tradition of quality color." He held up his copy. "There our flag flies, Old Glory in front of the post office, the orange, buff and aquamarine."

"Ya know," Yancy McWhirter, our mayor, said, "maybe what our great metropolitan weekly needs are a few kindly guidelines from interested citizens."

"Well, I'll tell ya what ain't important," Stafford Higginbotham said, "an' that's that San Francisco movie critic that thinks if a movie ain't made by a Frenchman or a Communist that it ain't worth watchin'. If I want symbolism I'll plug in a videotape of John Wayne wearin' an eye patch."

Vera Frudenburg, our third-grade teacher, harumphed. "While you're at it, throw out all those interviews with college football players. They shouldn't be allowed to speak more words than they've read."

"And throw away ever' interview by anybody named Ted," Corley said again. "We're caught up until about 1997 on quotes from Ted Kennedy, Ted Koppel, and Ted Turner. 'Course," he mused, "a few well-chosen words by Ted Williams would be nice."

Newt Jimson owns the Gas-N-Git convenience store out on the highway. "Lookee there, she done it again! It's the gas that's ninety-seven cents a gallon and the home-canned honey that's $1.49 a pint, not the other way around. Makes me look purely silly." He didn't hear somebody mutter, "T'weren't the paper that did that."

Everybody jumped as Leonard Ply slapped his paper on the cafe counter. "Instead of tellin' us how many's gonna go to their reward this weekend in car wrecks, whyn't they just make a guess about the number that's gonna overeat and croak from gastritis. Now, that'd be valuable."

Yancy stood. "Why don't we make a list for Dolly of dos and don'ts for our paper. Who's first?"

"Drop every reference to Cambodian rebels, Polish coal miners, or ladies' personal items." A big congregational "Amen."

"We need more coverage of America's new upsurge of interest in Wagnerian operas." Heads slowly swiveled toward Silas Eddardson, the owner and lone professor in the Cedar Gap Conservatory of Music. The echoing silence was enough to cancel that line on the blackboard.

IdaLou Vanderburg heaved herself out of her chair and headed for the Palace Cafe kitchen. "I'll tell ya, I don't care if that Russian Gorbachev does have a map of Florida tattooed on his bald head, I've heard enough about liver spots to last me the rest of my days."

Milo Shively shuddered. "Well, I'm real caught up on detailed lists of what it is that's clogging my kitchen drain lines."

"And drop all references to hog lice and goat parasites."

"How about if we just run articles about lost dogs that wandered back home and couples that managed to stay married more than forty-five minutes? Not much excitement, but . . ."

"An' pictures of the oldest hay baler in the county still running. My Uncle Henry's had that baler of his since . . ."

"Don't forget that gourd I grew that looks like Jimmy Carter," Milo said.

"That wasn't Jimmy Carter," Vera objected, "It was Jimmy Swaggart. You could tell by the little beady eyes and the tears."

Yancy quietly laid his chalk down and walked away. The Friday edition of the *Galaxy-Telegraph* that always arrives on Saturday had once again worked its magic: it produced an informed community.

Can you ask more from eight pages?

Talk It Like It Sounds, Y'all

A few days ago those two arbiters of fine taste in speech, Vera Frudenburg and Newton Jimson, sat glaring at each other in the Palace

Cafe. Vera, our third-grade teacher at the elementary school, holds to the classicist's view that what's right's right, and don't muddy the literary waters with mutant imagination. Newt's concepts of the English language, Texas derivation, runs more to the improvisational and ad hoc.

"Come on, Vera, you got your bun pinned too tight again. *We know what we mean by Tuesday week.*"

Vera's lantern jaw bulged. "If Cedar Gap were the center of the universe, then everybody would know it means a week from next Tuesday, but in Duluth it might mean anything or nothing. In a world that needs all the clarity it can find, it's just plainly confusing."

"Vera," Newt soothed, "you've never been to Duluth, and you won't get to Duluth unless you do some truly nasty things in your life and then get assigned there right after you die." He glanced around at his audience. "And it's for sure Duluth won't come here. What's the problem?"

"The problem is the same as when somebody says he'll be home at dark-thirty. Nobody knows what that means."

"Aw, c'mon, Vera," Newt chided. "We all know that means thirty minutes after sundown."

"Or after sunup!" Vera said, pointing.

"Naw," Yancy McWhirter said, shaking his head. "That'd be light-thirty."

"Let's get on a lower level," Vera said, her eyes pinpoints. "Use the word *mere* in a sentence."

Newt opened his mouth, but Corley Freemont jumped in. "Aw, 'at's an easy one. I 'member it from high school English class: 'Mere, mere on the wall, who's the fair'st of 'em all?' "

Vera's head jerked up triumphantly. "There you are, Newton! You've really got the literati working for you today. Luther, how about the word *tar*?"

Since Luther Gravely was sipping from the omnipresent straw stuck into the bottle in his coat pocket he missed his cue, but Leonard Ply snapped his fingers. "Glad you brought that up, Vera. I just noticed they's a flat on the right front tar of the Cedar Gap far truck."

Several heads nodded, appreciating the community information.

"Oh, this is wonderful," Vera muttered. "I teach in this town for twenty-seven years, and I just now realized that all the time I've had bilingual classes. I teach proper English, but everybody else in town speaks some bizarre jargon." She tore a page from a notebook, scribbled a few words, and handed the page to Yancy McWhirter. "Take this. I've got to get out of here. I can't stand that grinding sound."

Blank faces turned slowly. "What grinding sound?"

"The sound of William Shakespeare spinning in his coffin." Then she stormed out.

Everybody in the Palace Cafe looked a bit embarrassed. "I guess we hoorawed Vera a tad hard," Newton said. Then he grinned. "Read the words, Yancy."

Yancy tromboned the paper to get it in tune with his glasses. "Ummm, it looks like *rinch*." He peered over his glasses. "That's purty easy, but I guess we better do 'em all. Murph?"

"Piece a cake," Murphy Gumpton said, smiling widely. "I just got a new Maytag warsher in over at the Mercantile that's got a double rinch cycle." Then he frowned. "Or did you say *rainch*? If you did, it'd mean one a them funny little metric rainches Ambrosio uses to work on Jap cars. What's next?"

Yancy traced the list of words with his thick index finger. "How about *bobwar*?"

A quizzical look came on every face. "Yancy," Arnold Curnutt said slowly, "is Vera makin' fun a us? Ever'body knows what bobwar is. I been puttin' up bobwar fences since I could grap holt of a pair a plars. You sure she didn't mean *bubwar*, like an extension cord for a light bub?"

Newt grabbed Yancy's list. "Nope, *bobwar*'s the word she wrote, right after *sprang*."

Corley looked up. "That's that other pome: 'In sprang, a young man's fancy turns to thoughts a sangle girls.' "

Newt held up the list. "Look, Vera even wrote down *surl*, which I guess she means is that stuff kids 'n sissies eat for breakfast."

It was time for the cafe group to break up, anyway. Most of them figured if Anglish was being messed with, it was prob'ly the fault either a furriners or Big Bidness. It's enough to jist make you turn grain, hollar 'n thoe somethin'.

SATURDAY'S JOURNAL

HOUND-DOG NIGHTS

AND COYOTE MORNINGS

ell, it's a nice Saturday here in Cedar Gap, but for at least three people, the only thing that will get them up before Sunday morning is World War III or the Second Coming.

Yesterday Leonard Ply spied Bev Tolley coffeeing up at the Palace Cafe. "Hey, Bev, di'ja hear about that ol' boar coon Hig saw out on the mesa?"

Bev nodded. "Yeah. Said it was big as one a your shoats."

"I heard it was the size of a po-leese dog."

Bev muttered something about a first liar not having a chance. Then he said, "I'll tell you what. Whyn't you 'n me go up there tonight an' try to roust him out?"

"Tonight?" Leonard squinted at the ceiling. "Yeah, I guess I could . . ."

"HEY!" Bubba Batey leaned out from behind the Rockola jukebox. "Can I go with you guys?"

"Well, uh," Leonard hedged. He knew he had no reason to keep a reasonably ambulatory human from coming along on something as simplistic as a coon hunt. "Whatta ya say, Bev?"

Bev shrugged. He knew if Bubba had been born a piece of rope, he'd have been about three feet shy of long enough. "Aw, sure, I guess we can let him tag along."

"HEY, THAT'S GREAT," Bubba yelled. "I'LL BRING HAWK 'N SPIT."

Bev screwed up his face. "I don't know about your dogs, Bubba." Hawk and Spit, Bubba's two half-breed hounds, are about parallel with Bubba in the analysis department, meaning they rank someplace between crabgrass and a throw rug.

"AW, DON'TCHA WORRY ABOUT HAWK 'N SPIT! THEY'LL KEEP UP!"

Leonard shrugged helplessly. Maybe they could lose Bubba and his hounds in the darkness.

At two o'clock in the morning, the three skilled hunters took off up the mesa through the blackness. They walked for an hour until suddenly they heard, "Huhrooooon."

"HEY, THAT'S OL' SPIT!" Bubba yelled. "HE SMELLS COON!"

Bev listened, his head cocked. "You sure? That's not what I remember as a regular coon sound."

"YOU BET!" Bubba bawled proudly. "SPIT'S A BORN COONER. COME ON, HURRY UP! WE'LL LOSE 'EM!"

Bev and Leonard plowed through thorny shinnery and scrub cedar following what was now obviously the strident baying of two dogs. "OL' HAWK'S WITH SPIT!" Bubba yelled. "BOY, NOW YOU'RE GONNA HEAR . . ."

Suddenly, yelping and squalling filled the night while another squeaking sound moved back and forth in the darkness.

"Hey, Leonard, you hear that?" Bev asked. "Didja ever hear a coon squeak that way?"

Leonard listened. "Naw, never did. Don't they more like chatter?" He listened again. "You know, I believe I've heard that sound someplace before."

At that instant, something dark and snarling dropped from a low mesquite squarely onto Bubba's shoulders. Bubba staggered and lurched howling into a pile of dead leaves and prickly pear.

At Bubba's caterwauling shriek, Leonard and Bev grabbed in the dark for something harder than a fist. Unfortunately, all Bev could find in the blackness was a rotten fence post. He clutched the crumbling log and swung wildly at the snarling object just as Bubba stood up. The rotten fence post splintered against Bubba's shoulders, knocking the enraged animal to the ground. Bubba screamed and fell as if poleaxed.

"*Leonard, it's that boar coon!*" Bev yelled. "*Kill it!*"

"All I've got is a pocket knife! I'm leavin'!"

The three men leapt down the dark hill toward a narrow opening in the cedar that turned out to be a ten-foot free-fall into some loose shale. The coon, not all that much brighter, sailed into the pileup, clawing and chattering.

The three battered men yelled and threw rocks as they floundered down the steep mesa. Leonard stumbled through a rusty barbed wire fence, Bev almost lost an eye to a mesquite branch, and Bubba trampled both of them when he turned to yell for his dogs and tripped on a rock.

The sun was already up by the time they staggered into the Palace Cafe for some breakfast.

"Squeaking?" Ferrell Epperson asked. "You mean, sorta like that tailgate on Hig's propane truck?"

Bev nodded slowly.

"Aw, I'll betcha that was just Sybil's little feist out stirrin' up trouble. She's got the weirdest bark. Just like a rusty gate."

Leonard and Bev slowly swiveled their heads to frown at Bubba. "You mean," Bev said slowly, "all that noise an' fightin' was over a female dog?"

Bubba shrugged helplessly.

"Weeeeeeellll," Waldo Beeler said, "ever'body needs one a them hound-dog nights ever once in a while."

With a painful effort Bubba picked up his coffee cup. "It's the coyote mornin' that's about to kill me."

Everybody waited.

"Aw, you know." Bubba slowly stretched his shoulders, his face mirroring the pain. "That's where you feel like you been et by a coyote, and then puked over a cliff."

Every man nodded. Every man there had bought himself at least a couple of those mornings.

EPILOGUE

TO ALL THE YAHOOS WE'VE

LOVED BEFORE

ell, here it is Saturday again in Cedar Gap, and the assembly at the Palace Hotel and Cafe is in the process of redefining the term *yahoo*, which, by the way, is pronounced *Yay-hoo* to rhyme with *PAY-too*, as in *pay too much*.

A *yahoo* is generally thought of as someone who not only does something dumb, but does it automatically. It means either the acquired habit of being a jerk or the genetic propensity for jerkism, sometimes referred to by its medical name, *jerkus inheritismus*.

"You remember that yahoo down at Coleman who got drunk, then went out and tried to milk that ol' range bull?" Gunther Burns asked absently. "You could always tell in a dim light it was him because he walked kindly funny."

It was the cafe crowd's general consensus that yahooism was often inbred. "Aw," Waldo Beeler said, "I've seen it passed down through a family like bald heads or meanness. I mind that ol' boy, Hobart Something-or-other, from over at Baird who kept tryin' to teach his boy to hunt quail with a slingshot. Said his daddy taught him, and he wanted to pass it on to his boy."

"Either one of 'em ever hit one?"

"Not that anybody remembers, and that'll make three generations straight for yahoos in that one family."

To help with identifying potential yahoos, a short list of characteristics has been drawn up and certified as authentic.

- A yahoo always salts his potatoes before tasting them.
- A foreign yahoo thinks anything colder than room temperature is bad for the stomach. "You'll notice," Newt Jimson said, "those are usually the people who drink their beer warm and start lotsa wars." Leonard Ply nodded. "Somebody offered me a warm beer, I'd sure 'nuff start a war."
- A yahoo wears Reeboks with Levis and boots with plaid slacks and polo shirts.
- A pitiful yahoo—one for whom we truly feel great sorrow— considers moving to New York or Cleveland a step up.
- If he can spell Perrier, he's a yahoo. If he even thinks about drinking it, he's beyond help.
- One of the surest methods of spotting a closet yahoo is to give him something mechanical, and then watch how he works it. If he has to use both hands to open a bottle of soda pop, he's a yahoo.
- If he can't drive a stick-shift pickup, you can probably get papers on him and have him put away.
- Surefire test: You're riding along, the car gets a flat, and a normal human says, "Sit tight, this'll only take a couple a minutes." A yahoo looks confused and says, "I wonder what that flapping noise is? Think it's the carburetor?"
- Or, a red light goes on. When you stop, you find a broken fan belt on the ground. An average Texan says, "I got a spare in the tool box. This'll only take a couple a minutes." The yahoo picks up the fan belt and says triumphantly, "Here's the trouble! This little hose is all stopped up."

Common sense says there aren't just a whole bunch of female yahoos, but once in a great while you'll spot one. IdaLou Vanderburg, our sixty-five-year-old Palace Cafe cook, muttered, "Cookin's where it usually comes out in a woman. If her biscuits squat to rise, then bake on the squat, she's a yahoo. And if she cain't chicken-fry steak, just give up."

A girl yahoo tries to get her boyfriend to wear something other than cowboy boots with his three-piece suit to a wedding of a friend. Engaged Texas girls never try this because the boy always figures out what kinda girl he's going with and runs like a spotted ape.

Three final thoughts:

- A yahoo doesn't know the first line of "San Antonio Rose." It helps a little bit to be able to at least whistle the tune, but it's not something you'd be real proud of, either.
- Only a yahoo would name his boy Clive or Dirk, or his daughter Brandee.
- Any man who thinks there's a woman in the world better than his own mama is not only a yahoo, but he should be publicly flogged.

Thus, the Palace Cafe crowd decided that some people are born yahoos, others work to become yahoos, and some have yahooism thrust upon them.

Example: Some people believe there's no such place as Cedar Gap.

Such an attitude is pure evidence of the worst-case scenario: a brain-dead yahoo.

Pitiful!